JANICE ELLIOTT

Janice Elliott was born in Derbyshire and brought up in wartime Nottingham, the setting for her bestseller SECRET PLACES which won a Southern Arts award and was also made into a prize-winning film. She read English at St. Anne's College, Oxford, left a career in journalism for full-time writing in 1962 and now has twenty-two novels to her credit, her latest being CITY OF GATES. In addition to this volume of short stories, she has also written five children's books. Consistently acclaimed by the critics, she has been described as 'one of the best novelists writing in England'.

Janice Elliott and her husband now live in Cornwall which inspired her novel THE SADNESS OF WITCHES. For many years she was a fiction reviewer for the *Sunday Telegraph*. She is a Fellow of the Royal Society of Literature.

Janice Elliott

THE SADNESS OF WITCHES

Copyright © 1987 by Janice Elliott

First published in Great Britain in 1987 by Hodder and Stoughton Ltd.

Sceptre edition 1988
Fifth impression 1993

Sceptre is an imprint of Hodder and Stoughton Paperbacks, a division of Hodder and Stoughton Ltd.

Printed and bound in Great Britain for Hodder and Stoughton Paperbacks, a division of Hodder and Stoughton Ltd., Mill Road, Dunton Green, Sevenoaks, Kent TN13 2YA. (Editorial Office: 47 Bedford Square, London WC1B 3DP) by Clays Ltd., St Ives plc. Photoset by Rowland Phototypesetting Ltd., Bury St Edmunds, Suffolk.

British Library C.I.P.

Elliott, Janice, *1931*–
   The sadness of witches.
   I. Title
823'.914[F]

ISBN 0-340-43099-0

For Sheena and Donald Rickard

BELTANE

ONE

Martha Price sat at her window. She considered the blank pane. As she watched, the glass cleared. She raised her hand and there was the harbour. Two fishing boats steaming in. A yacht. On the other side of the water a small village climbed the steep hill to the cliff-top. A scattering of gulls in the mid-air.

She might have been a painter. Or a writer.

She pondered, considered the coastguard cottages crouched against the sky.

There was movement. A figure, then two or three. She nodded.

Let it begin.

So off they went to sanctuary, to a land by the sea of no frost where the air was made of light, the cliffs an hallucination, shaking in the ever-moving light. And as they came round the headland there, like God's finger, the sun stabbed through mist. Light when it was first made.

Then it rained. Both upwards and downwards, it seemed. The town on the other side of the bay was blotted out. Walter strode from the car park to the cottage clutching books as dear as babies to his chest. With his long gait and flowing locks, he had the air of an itinerant preacher arrived at last at his parish, awaiting his flock. Only sheep looked up. His wife Molly watched, loved him, she supposed, but wondered how she lived with a man who loved the world. Meanwhile, just for a moment, her hair fallen down and drenched into a tangle, she stood on the cliffpath and gasped at a small wonder: the hoop of a perfect rainbow blessing the bay.

'Oh!' said Gladys, coming up behind, long skirt trailing and the rabbit wrapped in her cloak, 'isn't it pretty then!'

Bother Gladys, thought Molly, she always spoils things.

Just as they turned to go in the veil of rain was swept aside and across the river in windows seemingly blind, binoculars were raised. In the club they nodded. The Watermans had arrived.

Three months ago in Wandsworth at the Watermans' home which had also been the Earthfolk headquarters, a brick was hurled through the window, the rates went up to £2000 a year, the electricity bill could not be paid and Walter, with unswerving integrity, refused to borrow from EF funds. They were accordingly cut off, the snow fell (isn't it pretty, said Gladys), Gladys's rabbit Hazel had to be brought indoors and Walter, Molly, Gladys, Hazel, and others concerned in the crusade to save the earth from death, shivered round a guttering candle and boarded windows, cooking by bottled gas.

Molly had cried three times in her adult life. Twice, when Penny and Tinker were born – and now a third time because the Butagas had run out. Gladys at the same time, reading the paper, informed them that there had arrived in England, disguised as a blackbird, the grey shrike, impaler of small birds.

'Isn't that a pity,' said Gladys.

Molly wiped her eyes and blew her nose.

'Walter, something must be done about it.'

Walter looked up. It was unusual for Molly to be fussed. His life in a way depended on the fact that Molly never fussed.

'I'm not sure we can do anything about that. One can't go round potting blackbirds.'

'I said we can't go on like this.'

'It seems to me more ornithologists' territory. You know the bird people don't like us to trespass. If it were a matter of pollution or crop-sprays . . .'

Penny was sitting in her rocker by the Furnacite stove, suckling her latest – twins; one pinned to each small but astonishingly bountiful breast.

'Pop, Ma isn't talking about birds. She means we've got to move.'

'Move? Where?' Walter was as startled as if his bed had been whipped from under him, the van arrived at the door. 'Why? But we've always lived here.'

Molly composed herself. 'Walter, we've lived in fifteen places in the last thirty years and you never noticed any of them. It's become expensive here and very unpleasant. I was thinking somewhere like the Cotswolds.'

In her mind's eye Molly could see the picture: the cottage of mellowed golden stone, an orchard in autumn light, Penny's children running barefoot, herself in a herb garden whose scent came to her with an intensity she seemed to be remembering rather than imagining, as though she knew her way in the dusk across flagstones, rubbing between her fingers the comfort of thyme and tarragon, rosemary and grey-leafed sage.

While Walter? Well, there might be consolation there even for him who appeared inconsolable: as who wouldn't be who witnessed the wreck of his beloved planet? Poor Walter. Yet Molly could remember him happy once, in a vegetable garden when they were young, dancing round his carrot patch, with an arm for her waist, his dark locks wild, his bearing triumphant – king of the veg. Oh, how they had made love that night!

The seed sown, Molly knew better than to press. Took deep breaths to calm herself, unearthed a primus in the attic and fried bacon and eggs, lit an oil-lamp, switched on the transistor and found Monteverdi on Radio 3. Gladys and Penny did a jigsaw puzzle, Molly knitted and Walter hummed – a signal from him not of content but of deep thought.

At four in the morning Molly woke. It was very cold and Walter was shaking her gently by the shoulders.

'What's wrong?'

'Nothing. Everything.' He stood over her, a blanket wrapped round his lean frame. 'I've decided. It's too late – for us anyway.'

Molly was confused. 'Too late? What time is it?'

'For the Earthfolk. We're giving it up.'

'Oh, love.'

'It's been too late for a long time. I didn't see.'

'But it's been your life. What will we do?'

'I don't know.' There was something glinting about him. 'Find sanctuary? In any case we're moving.'

'Oh, good. Where to?'

'West!'

He spoke with the air of an early navigator in search of virgin America, getting his first sniff of Martha's Vineyard. Such innocence must be blessed, Molly thought, though she recalled times when it had caused complications, embarrassment, near-disaster. At the Environment conference in Stockholm in the seventies it had been to say the least startling to find one's husband squatting outside the meeting hall naked but for loincloth and begging bowl. Just as well it was June. Yet, in part, she had married him for that, she supposed: his sadness and simplicity, his air of bewildered faith and features of a carved saint some-where between Sebastian and Francis – the latter Molly imagined, since she felt herself so often an inadequate Poor Clare. She loved him, but then there was nothing exceptional about that. Everyone loved Walter.

She reached for his hand.

'Come back to bed. I'm freezing. Where West? Oh, your hands are so cold!'

'Poltreth,' he said as she drew his head to her breast and pulled the duvet around them both. 'I remember it. I was there as a child. By the sea.'

They did not often make love now but tonight was clearly a celebration. Not for the first time Molly reflected the young can have no idea of the splendours of middle-aged love in a long marriage: familiar terrain revisited yet still surprising vistas. The richness. The sense of a continuing dialogue from the years piled up. Her fingers in Walter's wiry hair, Molly thought this is how Odysseus must have returned to Penelope, weary with time, grizzled, the sea in his eyes and ears; and she would count the scars and see him go again, greybeard, to battle.

Ah well, at least she could travel with him if only to carry his spears. They would be off, that seemed certain now; a decision had been made elsewhere, in the cave of time. She plucked her grandchildren from the soft garden of her dreams, gave them buckets and spades but could not yet perceive them on the beach. When she came to think about it she had rarely been to the seaside. That remained to be imagined.

While Molly lay awake Walter, landlocked Aquarius, stood by a pool that seemed to his child's eye the size of an ocean. A little fringe of tide curled round his bare toes and he laughed. Perhaps he was not a child but a dwarf, for he was aware in a way a child would not be of an immensity of waters, great oceans under the tug of the moon feeding seas, estuaries, creeks, pools. And these waters were mounting now, swirling around the small figure on the beach, and they were black.

Walter woke sweating. Molly wondered: 'How shall we start?'

'A nice cup of tea,' said Gladys.

'Yes, of course we'll come. For holidays anyway.'

Tess Allgood was speaking. She and Humph were the Watermans' oldest friends. Whither the Watermans went, there went Tess and Humph. It struck Molly sitting at the kitchen table with Tess, that she had over the years got into the habit of gratitude to Tess, not least for her competence. While Humph mended things in Walter's chaotic wake, Tess repaired situations. That was her job within the friendship.

Only for a second did Molly wonder how it might be without Tess and her tank-like common sense. Some friendships were like marriage. It would take a divorce to shake off the Allgoods. If she wanted to.

'And now we can afford it.'

Tess shook her head.

'Insane. All this time Walter had those shares. And you were scraping and half-starving. Had he really forgotten them?'

'His mother left them to him. But money's never meant anything to Walter. You know that.'

'Oh, yes. I know that.'

Humph had found the shares among the Earthfolk papers in a pre-war Oxo tin.

Tess sighed.

'Well, at least you can always be sure of Gladys.'

Molly realised how tired she felt. She made two cups of instant coffee.

'Yes, we can always be sure of Gladys.'

'Wherever did you find her? I've never known.'

'We didn't. She attached herself. She worked in a health food shop in Godalming. Walter was speaking and only two people turned up. Gladys was one. She's marvellous, of course.'

'Absolutely marvellous.'

Marvellous Gladys was at that moment talking to Hazel, her rabbit.

'We're going to live at the seaside. Won't that be nice?'

Hazel had pink eyes, white fur and a mobile nose. She was otherwise expressionless and sadly mute but Gladys liked to believe that she knew how much she loved her. Gladys had been aware all her conscious life that people found her boring and had never, therefore, expected to receive love; but at least she could give it: to God, to Walter and Hazel, if only by making herself useful. There were wells of passion in her, she knew, but doubted if anyone would ever come to draw a bucket there. She alone sensed her kinship to waters deep and strong. What a pity rabbits couldn't swim. Or could they? It was quite worrying, wondering if Hazel would adjust to her new environment.

Amazingly quickly it was settled. Walter and Humph Allgood made an excursion and returned with the lease of a coastguard cottage, extensive views harbour and sea, ideal for holiday/retirement/renovation. The Wandsworth house was sold to a property developer with planning permission to knock it down.

And so they sat, among packing cases, tea chests, the rubbish and treasures of years, by the light of an oil-lamp – Russians resting for luck before the journey, between lives. Walter dozed. Penny yawned. It all seemed a fuss about nothing to her, where you lived. The twins were asleep and Molly was reading to Penny's eldest, Jason, from the *Life* Young Readers Library.

'The earliest animal fossils so far found are those of primitive water-dwelling invertebrates – animals without backbones. Already they were quite advanced in structure. Some had jointed bodies and shells. They were in fact creatures well adapted to their environment, the ancient, silent seas.'

Jason wriggled. He was bored. Walter woke and smiled, alert. He might have heard a signal calling him to a new world. Assembling his wayward, jagged limbs, he went out for a walk in the rain.

Jason had been put to bed, demanding to know where they were going to live.

'At the seaside,' Molly said. 'You'll have a lovely time.'

'Will there be telly?'

'I expect so. But you'll find lots of other things to do.'

Jason looked doubtful. At seven, he was a middle-aged conservative.

'I like it here.'

'But you liked it at Shoreham last year. With Mummy and Stan.'

'Stan smells.' It was perfectly true, Molly thought; Jason's father, an itinerant jobbing plumber, did smell, not of drains as you might expect but of Caliban, something wild and feral – he had curls of black hair down his back. She was ashamed of the thought but shuddered when she imagined Penny's fair little frame crushed beneath such a speechless weight. Or perhaps they did speak, communicating in a private language of earth and fire and soil? 'Anyway that was holiday.'

Jason having made his point was at last defeated by sleep. He stuffed his fist in his mouth and kicked his teddy bear out of bed. Molly kissed her grandson, straightened his duvet and wondered, the bear clasped to her chest, how miraculously Penny's offspring seemed to survive her slapdash motherhood. Doubtless she was right and our generation wrong to fret so much. All had changed, the world had turned round and Molly wished with all her heart that it might be for the best.

Downstairs Penny had made coffee and seemed unusually inclined to talk. She sat on the floor in front of the stove, coffee undrunk, pale hair falling in wings to her narrow shoulders.

'Has Pops always been like this? Not noticing, I mean?'

'But your father notices everything.'

Penny shook her head. 'That's not what I meant.' She looked

away from Molly, prodded the embers of the dying fire. 'Has he always been a failure?'

Molly was shocked. 'Failure?'

'Well, the EF wasn't exactly a success, was it? Not like Friends of the Earth or Greenpeace? But it's been his life?'

'Yes.'

'What was he like when you met him?'

'Exactly as he is now. He never changes.'

'That's what I thought.'

'It's remarkable really. He's an exceptional man. I think he's one of the few good people I've ever known.'

'Mm.' Penny picked up her mug. 'I'll take this to bed. Well, night, Ma.'

'Goodnight, darling. Nothing's worrying you, is it?'

'Not a thing.'

When Penny had gone to bed Molly sat on even though it was late and growing cold, waiting for Walter.

TWO

The morning after their arrival the rain stopped. For once Walter slept late but Molly, waking early, put on the kettle and stepped outside. The cottage was perched on the spine of the hill, the front door and neglected garden looking down onto the harbour. That was the way they had come in last night but this morning Molly stepped from the back door and there it was, a spread of grass, the tumbling cliff and beyond as far as you could see, sea-sky, the horizon unmarked in the fragile early sun but miles and miles of light.

On the other side of the cottage she stood among the rubble and the grass run to seed, trees almost of tamarisk, and saw, as the mist shifted, the harbour begin to form. Across the water a church spire emerged, the chimneys of a big house on the hill; then a window here, a roof there, was sketched in until the mist cleared entirely and hulls that had seemed mastless were seen to be yachts, the town and quays were revealed and a stretch of villas almost as far as the point. Their gardens were terraced, windows signalled in the sun and a woman appeared to be feeding the seagulls that had woken Molly, crying like babies.

'Bloody buzzards,' said Martha Price, throwing a stone at the seagulls. 'Pounce, don't be daft. They'd eat you for breakfast.'

The small cat leaped down from the terrace wall, circled Martha's legs once, swore soundlessly and after a delicate and bored inspection of a tub of narcissi, settled in a puddle of sun. While all but the cliff-top houses in Poltreth were still in shadow, Poltrue basked all day until sunset when the windows over the water were suddenly fired and gold suffused the stones, the walls, the chimneys, the trees, and Poltrue sighed and slipped into dusk.

So, until sunset, Martha could be in the sun all day on her terrace in the house of many levels, the street above, below, shrubs and then rock staggering to the sea with the hazardous slippery steps to a shallow landing. At night at high water and spring tides she would hear the groan and crack of the sea in caves she had never entered and never could and she would lie awake, mouth dry and eyes bright. Each year – though not enough to measure – the sea rose, picking at the land, the rocks, Martha's house. She grinned, heaved Pounce off the bedspread and trailed to the basement where she would crouch and listen, ear to the granite, to the deep-throated voice of the sea.

They take me for mad, I daresay. A woman alone, burned almost black by midsummer, sallow all winter. Too thin, something threatening they find in my bones, my clothes, my gaze. Walk the cliffs, perch on my eyrie, an odd bird in strange plumage.

You should see what I can grow here in these few yards of soil. Fuchsia trees, a hedge of impatiens, hydrangea as vulgar as a bosomy barmaid; the violence of tiger lilies I don't care for but they refuse to die, spilling their black seeds in a conspiracy with the earth. The gentler heartsease fern and lavandula seed themselves in the stones and the stones themselves hold secrets: the imprint of a leaf or mollusc, fossils of other wilder gardens before the fall.

Last summer I saw a humming bird.

If I can write three hours this morning I can go for a walk or sail round to the bay. Will there be a wind?

Martha looked up at the sky, trying to guess the weather. A light breeze had come up, clearing the rags of mist. Someone else had got up early. There on the skyline of Poltreth were figures, one the size of a woman, the other a child.

In the Channel Hotel – the vast pink-washed statement of Edwardian complacence that stood on the highest point above Poltrue – Norah Carteret dressed stiffly and as silently as possible, not to wake Gerald. For a year or two now, ever since he had the small stroke and they moved here to the cheapest room, her husband's sleeps had frightened her, that he might nip off and leave her senseless, without a hand in a universe she had ceased to understand.

Silly old duck, she told herself, standing in a shower of hairpins, in such a fuss to get down first just for the newspaper that would keep Gerald happy or at least below boiling point.

At the landing window she paused and took a little breath. The sea never ceased to surprise her, as though like Gerald it might go out in the night and never come back. Well, they tell us daily the oceans are poisoned (the earth too) so that if we do not destroy ourselves, nature will turn against us.

Best to live on the surface of things, take the beautiful sea for what it appears; shaking flakes of light, a joy.

Was that someone standing against the sky outside the coast-guard cottage? The new people moved in? Perhaps they would be young. It would be good to have a little life around the place. Thirty years ago the room we have now was for servants, beyond our ken.

They were still vacuuming the big lounge with the palms and the picture window, the newspaper laid out on the piano. Norah smiled. Such a pretty room, she could have said, almost unchanged, with the only slightly faded red velvet buttoned banquettes, the chandeliers, the pillars covered in tiny squares of mirror glass and the mirrors themselves painted so that you saw both yourself and that lovely girl with the water-lilies who appeared, alas, to be drowning: at least it was hard to tell where her long hair ended and the clinging water plants began; she might be already underwater for bubbles rose around her, though there were stars too. Perhaps she was drowning in the sky?

Those mirrors had always affected Norah oddly, she remembered. She remembered dancing too in this room and an orchestra that had played for the Prince of Wales. Dancing and dancing and funny coloured drinks; and one night they followed the tall pale man with the saxophone out through the doors (no picture window then) through the gardens, down the road, and across the beach to the sea. Had someone tipped him? He went on walking till he was up to the waist and still playing, the tide

coming in, curling around our shoes, our ankles, the hems of
our skirts (the salt never came out, I could show you, I still
have the frock).

No one dances any more.

While Norah scuttled back to her burrow with the *Telegraph* for
Gerald's awakening, the kitchen staff who had clocked in an hour
ago were finishing their own breakfast. In his private flat the
manager ate his kipper and reflected on the season just begun.
The tariff had been revised but there would have to be further
economies. He was haunted by empty rooms. A good summer
would help. He looked out. There was a dash of rain on the
window.

The hotel had now woken and was breathing. There were
calls for tea (the Carterets had their own electric kettle and
Gerald's Darjeeling in that pretty tin from Jacksons years ago).
Early honeymooners whispered and made love again. Only in
the Ocean Suite the Principessa (born Annie Stubbs and as
Nancy Forrest a big star once) sank deeper into the drug-dreams
that would clasp her until noon at least. She would mumble and
mouth in threatening seas, reach out empty arms no longer filled
and laugh at old larks in ghostly company.

'Look, Jason,' Molly said. 'Isn't it beautiful?'

'Can we go on the beach?'

'I'm not sure where it is yet. We'll find it later.'

'Can we go now?'

'After breakfast.'

'Why are we living here?'

'Because it's peaceful. And London is horrid.'

'I liked London.'

How do you tell a child that the world has become a dangerous
place? Someone has left open a door and the planet is draughty.
It may be there is no sanctuary anywhere, even here. But one
lives. One clings to life, smaller things. Look down and see how
the garden grows. A flower, a snail, a shell. Well, of course we
don't tell the children.

Molly took her grandson's hand and turned back towards the

cottage. A breeze had come up and she felt chilled in her thin clothes. The light had gone out of the sea.

The coastguard cottage gazed with one eye upriver, the other out to sea, though it no longer kept watch. The idea of the unscanned waters worried Molly when she thought of it, as she did now, watching from the upstairs window a fishing-boat thump out over the now flurried waves. All done by radio nowadays, Humph Allgood said, but she could not wipe from her mind the vision of silent wrecks. The shivers, she decided, morbid. One could no longer flit so lightly after all from one life to another. There must be a pause, a time to let go as the new world formed. And this place surely was like none she had ever known: another country. Molly touched the back of a familiar chair, fingered her wedding ring. Mutability, she thought, and continuity – the first an inescapable condition of life, the second such a fragile thread. What courage it would take to let it go.

Did men feel this? She had no idea. There was Walter in the strip of garden crouched with Gladys before Hazel's cage. They were considering the rabbit with greatest seriousness. Yes, Molly concluded, Walter was all right: he had his Walterness.

His selfishness too, Penny had hinted more than once, fond though she was of her father. But what did Penny know, or anyone else, of the Walter Molly loved? In the secrecy of marriage, that private chamber where none but the couple enter, Molly understood how stricken he often was, how much he yearned to give the extraordinary passion he had in him, in ordinary ways. But it was as though he had emerged upon the earth as an orphan, never learned the human tricks. Over the years she had helped him. He had tried. And there had been glorious occasions when he reached out from what she saw as not his selfishness but his loneliness, and they had been quite simply happy together in a way no one else could be expected to understand.

There he was now with his arm round his grandson's shoulders, turning and smiling as Molly walked across the place that would be a garden, to join him.

'Beautiful,' Walter said and ducked his face to kiss her.

'Yes. Even more than I'd expected.'

'No. You. You are my beautiful wife.'

They stood together, watching Jason run.

Walter said: 'I'm sorry.'

Molly put her finger to his lips. She wanted to hold this moment.

'Hush.'

'Look! There are the Allgoods.'

Tinker arrived with Tess and Humph in the hired pantechnicon, swaying perilously as it rounded the hill and took the turn to the public car park. From there they would have to unload, the men heaving what they could carry, either on their shoulders or transferred to a wheeled trolley, while the women sorted the lighter objects: some for the coastguard house, some for the Allgoods' rented cottage by the Mission Church. Molly ran to meet them. She was amazed to find she was crying.

Tess grinned. 'There, love. We're only an hour late. There was a bomb scare. They were diverting round Streatham or somewhere. What's it like then?'

'Lovely. I don't know.'

'Well I do. I want a toddy. You do the tea. I'll do the Scotch.'

'Yes, of course. I'll put it on. The tea, I mean.'

Tinker seemed immense in the small kitchen, his Walter-elbows jagged, his head ducked to avoid the ceiling. So, in the month since Molly had seen him, he had grown from her. Away? No, never, quite. It was simply that in the last year a metamorphosis had taken place, his face had thinned, muscles hardened, he had put on the body of a man. He had grown too large for her arms. His cheek was rough to kiss.

'Well, what do you think?'

'Fine. It's all right.'

Now there were too many people in the kitchen: Molly, Tess, Gladys, Humph, Tinker, Penny, Jason; Walter blinking in the doorway looked ready to bolt.

'Everyone who can, sit down.' Molly found kettle, tea bags, mugs, Marvel, no sugar. Tess was slopping in the whisky.

'Enough of this, they'll never notice.'

'Not Jason. And I don't think Gladys drinks.'

'She does now.'

Tess grinned. The fug thickened but it was better now. Tinker was squatting in a corner, his knees up to his chin. Someone had found chairs. Darkness had come down suddenly, curtaining the windows. It was a comfort. Humph had got the stove going. Molly raised her glass. Well here we are then.

Walter had bolted. That is to say, he had never quite come into the crowded room and now, with a half-wave of his hand, in case anyone noticed, he was off, striding away from the room, the light, the warmth, the house, across the grass towards the path he had noticed by daylight. Anyone else would have paused to admire the moon on the water, the chapel ruin, the distant silvered headland, but views were not for Walter. He used to wonder, absently, if he were missing something. Did it worry Molly, this blindness of his? Look, she would say as they reached the summit of a hill or came upon a wide valley and he would gaze but he could not share it. So their long marriage took on a certain shape. There were the children, the work, and when there was a chance Molly set out with her stool and pad and paints while Walter walked alone with his vision which lay in a crinkle of the earth, a pebble, a beetle, a fly released from a spider's web. But most of all the aqueous – a raindrop in a glass dish, a shining puddle on a London pavement, and now the sea. The fish that swam in it, the creatures temporarily beached with the tide's ebb; and since they had come here intimations even of something larger he could not yet grasp but that drew him away from his hearth down the track to the sea.

There were tricks on the path. Although Walter's night-vision was still good gorse bushes snagged his clothes, hidden pitfalls turned his ankle and the slippery route, seeming to lead one way, would veer at the last moment in another. Halfway down, screened from the top, was a small stone building so far as he could see abandoned. Was that a shadow following him or a cloud across the moon? Walter shook his head, slithered and stumbled on, down, all the time alert to an increasingly peremptory call, a voice raked across stones; alternately full in advance and hoarse in retreat: the sea.

At the last moment he tripped and in a clatter of shale fell and lay for a moment panting. The black dog that had picked its way after him from the hut did not yet care to approach but squatted on its sharp haunches a few yards from the forked creature on the beach. When the figure moved the dog edged back a little, soberly observing as the man took off his shoes then his sweater, shirt and trousers and walked into the sea, breasting the small waves, swimming wildly at first for warmth, then more steadily until twenty strokes or so from the shore, he disappeared. The dog whined faintly in his throat and paced the edge of the tide until the man surfaced, laughing, shaking scales of phosphorescence from his limbs.

By the light of an oil-lamp, on the other side of the bay, Martha Price shared a small mackerel with Pounce, who complained that it was not smoked. Stupid fleabag, I'll put out dog-food if you don't shut up. If I could afford it. If I had credit in town any more. Rats are too large to catch, of course, they'd swallow you up head first then crunch-crunch to the tail. Mummy caught a fishy for her little pussy and the beast won't eat it.

You know what they used to do round here? Put kitty in a sack and chuck him off the cliff. Maybe still do.

Martha scraped the mould off a corner of cheddar and chewed it up to the rind. One wrinkled apple. Half a bottle of plonk. Scotch in the cupboard, there must be one left, but living alone best lay off spirits or we'll be the town drunk won't we, Pounce. Poor puss, Martha's bark is worse than her bite. You know that if no one else does.

Living alone. Bad and good. The voice furs up in the throat and comes out as a growl, a smile as a grimace, children play grandmother's footsteps in my wake; and although my ordinary need for company has atrophied I miss touch. Not merely in a sexual way – by no means – but the ordinary exchanges of the flesh. My arms are empty.

Good – I hurt no one but myself. Also, solitary, I am fully alert. Senses untrammelled, I can receive, perceive. Colours cry aloud, sound takes on the wildest colours and scent carries urgent messages. More particularly I spy secrets. I am a reader of other people's telegrams of distress – the anxious smile of the old duck from the Channel Hotel with the wonky husband, how her hand shakes when she buys an expensive nectarine she will take to the ferry shelter, pare with a child's penknife and devour alone. I am not cold or mad. She touches me.

What a moon, the colour of fish-scales. I am still capable of wonder. I can still say: I am.

Where was Walter? Would he fall down the cliff? Should they look for him? Leaving, kissing Molly, pausing at the door, the Allgoods fretted. Solid Humph had the instincts of a St Bernard; he would if he could have retrieved everything lost, hurt, in peril, and the cliffs were dangerous.

'No,' said Molly. 'No, look, the moon's come up.'

Walter had dressed and was warming himself jogging on the beach. He threw a stick for the dog. He was not aware of the moon, only that he could see as clear almost as day. Puffed, he sat on a rock, shivering a little still but more exhilarated than he could remember for years. There go the ships and there is that Leviathan. Surfacing from oceans of forgetfulness, a few words spoken in school chapel on a warm summer evening in his days of vocation. That is to say, when there was still a presence calling from the bell-tower, occasionally from the singing dimness of the organ loft: come to me. And secretly and with longing the boy had answered Yes.

What a simple answer it had seemed. Somewhere to fit in, someone to talk to for the awkward adolescent who felt himself ill-equipped for both school and world. For Walter had wondered fervently then and even still vaguely, what it meant to be human. He considered now that it was not perhaps such a grand thing, but then how could he know if he was excluded? And how painful it had been for the boy trying to learn the tricks. Easier to be Waterman the odd-bod, creeping Jesus, clown it up, grin when they catch you on your knees or they'll shove your face in the lavatory-pan. A hot embarrassed tea with the chaplain.

Masturbate much, Waterman? Nothing to be ashamed of. God might have been acne, a stage you go through and grow out of.

And so he had. Or rather at some point He had left. That is not to say died but simply removed His presence (grown out of Walter perhaps?), leaving him desolate to creep upon the face of the earth, a dung-beetle carrying a burden of love. Molly, of course. Yet even then, loving her – in a way, the more he loved her – he could touch her face and wonder if human love were not a poor image of the divine. Walter still lived with his ear cocked for a voice. Perhaps now, if he listened? Certainly there had been a summons tonight which accounted for the fact that he was now sitting on a rock grinning foolishly in the moonlight. The only question was who or what had called?

'Lovely night.'

Looking out to sea Walter had not noticed the rower resting on his oars a few yards from the beach. No, not his, her – though an odd-looking she, shapeless and somehow pointed around the head. Walter's first reaction was for flight but even he could hardly leap and run like a burglar. The dog which had been squatting beside him was now standing up to his haunches in the sea. He uttered a short warning bark. Walter stood. The woman showed no sign of beaching the dinghy but dipping her oars now and then kept her station. The pointed head, Walter now realised, was an eccentrically shaped oilskin hat. Otherwise, he could discern little about her beyond her dim shape against the silver water. He wasn't sure what to make of the peculiar situation and wished she would either land or go away.

'Was it you I saw swimming?'

'Yes.'

'Braver man than I.'

'I enjoyed it.'

'Ebb,' she called. 'Filthy. Only emmetts swim there.'

'Emmetts?'

'Trippers. You'll probably be all right if you didn't swallow any. I see you've got old Enoch.'

'Enoch?'

'The dog.'

'Oh yes, of course, the dog. Actually, he seems to have got me.'

Walter thought uncomfortably it was rather like being cornered at a party. He could not leave the beach until the woman went away. He was never able to think of anything to say at parties either.

'Well, we'd better get back before it runs too hard.'

Now he came to look at least three yards of muddy sand had appeared since he arrived. Although the water close to the beach was unruffled, further out it was troubled by patches of argumentative current as though great creatures turned in their sleep. But the woman was rowing well without any suggestion of effort. She waved once and as her dinghy crossed the Jacob's ladder Walter could have sworn he saw some animal sitting in the bows. A cat?

The swim and the strange meeting had tired Walter. The exhilaration of his wild dip had not entirely left him but it was a struggle back up the cliff path; making a few feet then slipping back, clutching at tufts of grass, he was convinced that somehow he had taken the wrong route or the track had changed. The moon went behind a cloud and abruptly Walter was robbed of sight and direction. Blinded, tearing his fingernails, groping for a foothold, he was clinging to an outcrop of rock when something screamed in his face and wings scythed the air around his head creating a kind of insane turbulence of which he was the centre and victim. With no hand free to lash out he could only press his face closer to the cliff imagining all the time his eyes plucked out by those hooked beaks.

Then as suddenly as they had set up their panic the gulls fell away carrying their clamour out to sea and from somewhere above Walter heard a short peremptory bark. He could see nothing but with a great effort forced himself up and away from his precarious toehold in the direction of the bark. The moon reappeared, the animal – if it had been there – was gone, but Walter saw that he was only a couple of steps from the true path – in some way that seemed to him miraculous he had been saved.

At the top he rested for a moment to recover himself then

set off for the cottage. As he closed the door behind him a black shadow detached itself from the night and settled down by the water-butt in the small back yard.

THREE

From her eyrie – mental as well as physical – Martha Price had come to see the life of the harbour as an ever-changing web of great intricacy. The ferry that ran just inside the harbour mouth connected smug sunny Poltrue with dark Poltreth. There it went now, while a yacht going out crossed its stern wave and a fishing-boat steamed in. In the mid-air and above, gulls set up a reflecting mesh of ceaseless movement. Once early in the morning on a still day Martha had seen a single swan proceed upriver, trailing a wake that fanned from shore to shore.

It was an occasional fantasy of hers that she could control this toy world: capsize the trippers' mosquito-buzzing hire-boats, reverse the wind and fill that spinnaker, lift the roofs from houses and peer inside on secrets and treasures and woes; summon a gale, set off the maroon and send the lifeboat dashing out. (Perhaps she could? She could.)

Not today. She felt benign after last night's row in the moon-shine. She reached for the binoculars and focused on the ferry.

At Poltreth Norah Carteret stepped ashore, a little shaky but at the last moment rejecting the ferryman's hand. For this was an act of daring and rebellion that had been forming in her mind since last night's moon. Perhaps it had turned her brain a little? More specifically, she and Gerald had dined, as they always did once a week, always a Wednesday, in the dining-room (normally they picnicked like mice in the evening after a cheap lunch at the Yacht Club). Their weekly binge – as Gerald referred to it – took place on a Wednesday because that was the day for liver. Norah did not like liver (however well cooked she could never forget the sight of it raw, blueish-brown and somehow still throbbing with blood), yet as ever on a Wednesday she had put on her next-to-best dinner frock, the good pearls, the uncomfortable shoes and the Yardley's rose lipstick to which she had reverted when the outline of her mouth had begun to shrink and wander. As they made their way into the new dining-room (full harbour view) Norah was struck disloyally by the fact that Gerald's failing memory retained yet the certainty of liver Wednesdays when he had forgotten his dead mother's name, those of his living children and on occasion hers. Not that he used hers much anyway. Their conversations were mostly a tentative one-sided essay on her side to which the response was normally a grunt. Still, Norah continued to talk to Gerald because it seemed to her important. Perhaps he did respond at some level – there were times when she caught in his small reddened eyes the look of someone locked in a room. Besides, this keeping up of any connection, however tenuous, struck Norah as vital, for herself as much as for him. She could not have said if there was love still between them but there was half a century and that might be more significant. They were joined by the fibre, muscles and nerves of habit and it alarmed her to imagine that this shared organism they had, their marriage, could ever be destroyed; though unless they were both to nip off in the night, she knew that some time it must.

So they sat at their out-of-season table in the window (come May and they would be banished to the corner by the serving-door) and Norah said, wasn't it pretty, the view of the lights at Poltreth, she gathered some new people had moved into the coastguard cottage. She touched her pearls and smiled and tried to swallow the liver without chewing or tasting but tonight she was more than usually aware of her throat constricting against the viscous lumps and of the blood on Gerald's plate. And then she saw the moon and looked at Gerald with his fork halfway to his mouth and in that second disliked him.

And now here she was, wobbly from the crabwise climb but breathlessly triumphant, an old woman in a Burberry and knitted hat sitting on a comfortably rounded granite rock outside the Watermans' cottage.

'We can't keep him,' Molly was saying, 'he could be anybody's dog. They might be looking for him.' But already she knew they would keep the dog because it was there, sitting under the eaves by the water-butt where it must have sheltered all night. So far it had made no attempt to enter the house. It seemed neither hostile nor friendly, except towards Walter. As soon as he came out to join the meeting around the dog it rose to greet him. Not a grovelling dog but a watching, careful one. And according to Walter it had saved his life or at least his limbs, though Molly had not yet made out what Walter had been up to climbing the cliff in the middle of the night. All she knew was that she had turned over in her sleep, kissed his cheek and half-woken long enough to say: 'You taste of salt.' She had sweated through some dream she could scarcely remember that he was in peril, coiled in the arms of a sea-monster, ensorcelled, drowning and then rescued. Tess always said that nightmares of someone else in danger were an expression of fear for oneself but then Tess admitted that she rarely dreamed so how could she know? Molly too had read her Jung. The sea can make you whole or send you mad. Well, that remained to be seen. Meanwhile, there was the matter of the dog, about which they all seemed to have become a little insane. It did look hungry though not exactly starving and of course it would be good for Jason.

'Poor dog,' said Gladys, and that was apparently it.

'Can I take him for a walk?' Jason was ecstatic.

'If you keep well away from the edge. And don't be long.'

Molly had found a baffling heap of Walter's clothes, damp and dirty and in one place torn. As she hung them on the line an odd little figure approached her, wispy grey hair escaping from a cap that might have been bought at a jumble sale.

'A lovely day,' said Norah Carteret. There was an air of fragility about her and also of bravado. 'It was so beautiful I thought I would come across. You know on a clear day you can see the Lizard from here.'

Lizard? For a second, putting on the last peg, Molly was

confused, back in her dream of creatures from the deep.

'Across?'

'From Poltrue.' She seemed friendly and anxious, as if at any moment she might run away. 'I try to come every year to see if the Spring Squill is out. The scilla, you know.'

'Of course.' Molly looked at her more closely. She would have been pretty once. At the moment she appeared out of breath. 'Would you like a cup of coffee?'

'Oh no. Thank you. Well. Yes, I would. That would be very nice, if you're not too busy.'

Molly smiled. She was reminded of some animal in one of Jason's books. Grey Rabbit? Mrs Tittlemouse?

'I'll bring it out – we're such a muddle indoors. Do sit down.' Molly indicated a bench at the edge of the yard, screened from the wind by the wall of the outhouse.

It was pleasant there, high above the dark, steep village, with the sun on their faces. Conversation did not seem urgent. They watched Jason running with the dog.

'I see you've found Enoch.'

'Oh – you know who owns the dog?'

'No one really. I'd say he's not the sort of dog anyone owns. Well someone did once naturally but he's been by himself for quite a while now.'

'But where does he live?'

'He uses that hut – just there where the path turns, can you see it? – he shelters there and people feed him. Everyone knows Enoch.'

'Oh good, then we haven't stolen him. We've just moved in you see.'

'I know.' Norah nodded. 'I'm afraid nothing stays private here for more than five minutes. You must be Mrs Waterman.'

'Molly. My husband's indoors and my son and daughter are around somewhere. That's Gladys feeding her rabbit.'

The coffee had perked up her visitor. She had more colour in her cheeks and seemed less shy.

'I'm Norah Carteret. We live over there in the Channel Hotel. Quite a little room. I mean I live with my husband. He doesn't get out very much. He's not so well, you see.'

'I'm sorry. Not serious, I hope?'

'At first they said nominal aphasia. Now they call it Alzheimer's disease.'

'I'm afraid I've never heard of that.'

'Neither had I. It means loss of memory. Premature senility. Apparently as it progresses you forget everything. In the end you remember nothing at all.'

'How terrible.'

Norah pondered. 'I wonder. The old live too much in the past, you know. It might make it easier to leave?' She put down her cup. 'Well, I must be off. I'm playing truant, to tell you the truth.'

Molly stood. 'I hope we meet again.'

'Oh we shall, we shall. Everyone meets everyone here. Except the Principessa – she's been in the Ocean Suite for thirty years now. She was once quite a famous film star. But I'm glad you've come, my dear. It will be good to have some younger blood. Shake us up a bit. We get pop stars sometimes but that's not the same.'

The two women stood gazing across the cliff to the sea. There was Jason, just in sight. The gorse was still tight-budded but tipped with honey.

Norah said suddenly, 'What do young people think? Will they drop the bomb?'

Molly understood – such beauty and such danger. She shook her head and called after Jason even though he could hardly have heard her: come back don't go too far.

Did I talk too much, Norah wondered? But it was such a treat to have someone listen. A nice young woman. Was one too old to make friends? She rested for a moment on her stick. Life could still be astonishing. Yesterday it was liver Wednesday and now here she was, having crossed the water, climbed the hill and met a stranger.

She knew exactly where she would find the scilla, on the slope down to the Combe, by the spring. Each year the downhill path became more difficult. Norah recognised her irresponsibility –

if she were to fall and no one find her and Gerald be left alone; but she would have this, her pilgrimage.

The gulls seemed noisier than ever this year. One flew in her face and she waved her stick. By the time she reached the spring she was dizzy and breathless. She sat on the end of the wooden footbridge and closed her eyes. When she opened them the thin figure of a girl in a long blue skirt, with bare feet, not very clean, had emerged from the thickening copse and was looking down at her.

Tinker had gone for beer and pasties. A veil of rain had swept in and dashed upriver and Molly and Penny sat indoors among the muddle of furniture. The twins were yelling but Penny was totally absorbed, picking thorns from the soles of her feet with Molly's tweezers.

'I found a funny old thing – a woman in a sort of heap, over there where the trees finish and you go down to the beach.'

Molly looked up from sorting books. Though what was the point without shelves to put them on? It was a slow job anyway because she kept stopping to read. They had never lived anywhere long enough to put their library in any kind of order and in a way Molly didn't want to – it was always fun seeing what would turn up: a kind of domestic archaeology. Iris Murdoch's *Flight from the Enchanter* – a very old Penguin with a dead spider inside; an Italian phrasebook; *Be Your Own Accountant* still stiff and unread from an improbable day when innumerate Walter was seized by the urge to set their finances straight – as unlikely as controlling the weather; *Silent Spring* with the corners of pages turned down and a shopping-list bookmark: baked beans, mungo sprouts, brown rice, Tampax, Smarties; and the Heinemann 1935 edition of Masefield's *The Box of Delights*. Well, that was a find! *In darkest Cellars underneath/Blood-hungry Sea-Wolves snap their Teeth.* Shudders and a pleasure whose tingle she could feel now.

'Sorry, darling, what did you say? What old thing? What was she doing?'

Penny yawned and, bringing her big toe to her mouth, sucked it – a double-jointed feat that always astounded Molly.

'Well, at first she seemed puffed, I thought she might be having a heart attack or something, then she perked up and rambled on about something called a siller. Then when I went away I saw her drinking from a sort of stream, with her hands. What is it anyway? A fish? There wouldn't be a fish up there, would there?'

'It's a flower that comes out at this time of year. Blue, the sort you get in ordinary gardens but I think this is a special one. And that was Mrs Carteret. She had coffee with me. Are you sure she was all right?'

'Oh, I should think so. Just a bit weirdo. It must be awful to be old,' Penny concluded cheerfully. The twins had begun to bawl but she seemed undisturbed.

Molly sat on the floor, Masefield still in her hand. 'I should think the worst thing is probably that you still feel yourself inside. I mean young. But stuck with an old body.' Penny wasn't listening. Oh well, that's what the young do. Halfway through a conversation, you think you're talking and they switch off.

As Penny changed the twins on the kitchen table Molly was struck by her daughter's grace and how easily she lived in her fragile-seeming body; how she lived in the world, for that matter, as though life were simply a country she had found herself in and she looked round and said, Oh, that's it, is it? It occurred to Molly that in spite of her casually acquired and delivered offspring (her longest labour had been four hours), the bare feet and indifference to clothes and appearance (most of her wardrobe was ten-year-old Oxfam), Penny was by nature a conformist. Even her spasmodic involvement with protest movements was carried out with the air of someone obligingly fulfilling a social duty – much as another class of female might turn out on a winter's night to attend a WI slide-lecture on flora and fauna of the Seychelles. Molly remembered catching a glimpse of her one rainy afternoon in Grosvenor Square when the Americans had done something they ought not to have done or had left undone those things which they ought to have done, squatting on the pavement outside the Embassy with a placard in her hand and a newspaper over her head. Her expression was that of someone putting up politely with rotten weather at a picnic. She had even been carried away once and spent a night in a cell. Molly had worried but Penny emerged the next day untouched – she appeared simply not to have noticed her surroundings. Jason had been conceived in a plastic bag Penny and Stan had shared one summer on Salisbury Plain.

Well at least, Molly thought, Penny is likely to stay, if only because to go would demand the kind of effort she seemed disinclined to make. Tinker, on the other hand – now stooping to get through the door with his cans of beer and Coke, Gladys and pasties bringing up the rear – had left the familial roof early and since then rarely spent more than a couple of nights beneath it before he was off again. Of the two the happier child and certainly the more demonstrative, he had got his two A-levels, hugged his mother, embraced his father and simply walked out with a pack on his back. When Molly recalled the scene she saw it as one of those turn-of-the-century paintings. A Collier perhaps, entitled *Leaving Home* or *The Parting*, it would depict Tinker sporting a cloak and Phrygian cap with a hooked staff and pouch at his waist containing bread, cheese and a sovereign, at the moment of turning to stride down the garden path; while in the cottage doorway stood framed she, Molly, shawled and bravely waving, with Walter at her back, stooped in the honeyed shadow. The fact that the Wandsworth house boasted, in place of rural path, rusty railings and a couple of overflowing black plastic refuse bags failed to tarnish Molly's picture. But then being of an allegorical turn of mind, she had never had any trouble finding sermons in stones. The trouble here was that the air seemed, if anything, overloaded with messages. She had expected to be lulled. Instead she was electrified. That odd little woman this morning. Whatever Walter had been up to last night. The dog. Something in the air.

Tinker laid out the lunch. This afternoon he would put up bookshelves with a deftness and speed that always startled his mother. But then he was, she supposed, a carpenter – or rather carpentry appeared to be one of his many peripatetic occupations. That was how he had met Stan, the travelling plumber, and brought him home. And Stan had eaten vast amounts of bread and dripping and taken Penny to set up a temporary household in a plastic bag and begat Jason who was running in at the door now, his cheeks flushed with air.

Tinker said: 'Glad had a cider in the pub, didn't you Glad?' Tinker was nice to Gladys. He took notice of her as no one else did – an attention that always brought her out in a flush that extended from her neck to the roots of her gingery hair. Not for the first time Molly was ashamed of her impatience. Even Gladys couldn't help having ginger hair and eyebrows and that particular, slightly acid smell of ginger people. It was shocking really how much relationships – or Molly's at least – were ruled by chemicals. Molly could detect the presence of her children, and now of Jason, in the dark. When Walter was away she would take a shirt of his to bed and press her nose to it. *The ass in the desert sniffs up the wind of his love.* Now where had she read that? She couldn't remember but she knew what it meant.

Tinker was saying that the pies were hot. They had been to two pubs: in one the natives were hostile, in the other friendly. The beer was good and the cider was great. There were three Methodist chapels (two in process of conversion to garages). Marvellous windows. He could have sworn one was a Rossetti.

'The place is empty. As if there'd been a plague.'

'Well, the season hasn't started, I suppose. A lot of them will be holiday lets. I expect Poltrue will be busier.'

'Where's Pa?'

'Gone over to the Allgoods. I think.' Come to that, where was Walter? Molly felt a flash of irritation. It had been the same with every move they made, from the bedsitter in the Fulham Road to the houseboat off Cheyne Walk thirty years ago, the disastrous Essex cottage, Islington before it got posh, Wandsworth – every time they packed up and moved on Walter behaved after the first mild outrage as if the whole business had nothing to do with him, even though it might have been his idea in the first place. He would either disappear or be present in only the most shadowy sense until his bed was made, the house in order, and then he would return with the air of a dispossessed dog looking for its basket. Yet in another sense he was spiritually roofless. While Molly knew herself to be a nester she could see Walter quite happy as a mendicant friar (that would be where Tinker got his wandering ways). She could even imagine that one day, like those Indian husbands, he might shed his few worldly goods and walk calmly away from them all. Although in a way she must always have known this, Molly only this second truly understood it so that she was startled as if a picture of her marriage had been held up to her and she had been forced really to look.

All this Molly was thinking while she unwrapped pasties, found a few plates, couldn't find forks, explained to Jason yes, he could drink from the can but no, there were no straws, yes, Tinker would fix the telly this afternoon (oh Lord, was there an aerial, she hadn't looked), wished suddenly in the middle of her family for a cup of tea and silence, sleep, a cool pillow in an airy room with white curtains lifting their skirts in the breeze.

I want, she thought, poised in the centre of her busyness – and then she did not know what she wanted except that words came into her mind like visiting angels: virgin, quiet, white, empty, peace, time. And the words were coloured. Time had the blue-white of fresh snow, an untouched field stretched boundlessly before her; quiet, light seen through fragile porcelain and peace the bloom of a golden apricot. She rocked slightly on her heels and at the same moment or perhaps a little before something was flung or flung itself against the window, a shock as if someone had shouted in her face. Then Penny was saying something.

'Ma, you've dropped the plate. It's smashed. Look. The one with roses on.'

Penny pointed. It was Tinker who picked up the bits.

'Not too bad. Could be mended.'

Molly heard herself say, 'What was that noise? Is the window broken?'

Tinker sat her down. That is, he grasped her gently by the shoulders and she found she was sitting down.

'Only a gull. They throw themselves against the windows. They seem to know when there are people inside.'

Molly looked. Yes, there was a smear of white on the pane. Nothing broken except for the plate but the sound of the bird on the glass had imploded inside her head. She blinked, steadied and took in where she was, at the table, with her family. Their faces ceased to waver, Jason was watching her with open curiosity. The twins were kicking and gurgling in their double carry-cot. Tinker said again: 'It can be mended.'

Yes, of course the plate could be mended, everything was as it should be, the window was not broken. But something had happened.

Norah said to Gerald: 'I found the Scilla Verna but it had a fungus. The petals wouldn't open properly. Did you know it's supposed to be a simple against moon-magic? When the moon's on the wane it keeps Hecate away. Oh well, I met a nice woman and I saw a strange girl.'

They were sitting before the gas fire on each side of the Benares brass table-top that could be lifted from its folding legs and put away. They were eating their late afternoon snack: roes on toast. Once this was the time of day when they would have sat with drinks in their hands, speaking or not speaking. There might have been friends, company, and years ago laughter, gossip, the swish of silk, scented air. Orchids, thought Norah, as tall as trees. Talk of home as a bird screeched beyond the mosquito screen. Dreaming of home. And now their exile was ended and it was home that had proved a dream, the sad kind from which one would prefer to awake.

After the morning's escapade she had missed lunch at the club and since she was not there to conduct him, so had Gerald. She had braced herself for disgrace but after all he had not reproached her. Perhaps he had simply forgotten her, along with lunch and the club. He had seemed even puzzled to see her and ever since her return had worn the same expression of faint bewilderment as if he were trying to identify her. No, it was more as though he were awaiting some message. Whatever it was, she had clearly failed to deliver it.

He opened his mouth as if to speak and Norah thought, now, he is going to tell me, to say it, to ask, and she watched the struggle of his mind in his eyes. It struck her, if the past has gone and he has so little present, where does his poor mind live? The soul, if it existed, she had always seen vaguely as something like a moth that fluttered from the body on death and might, she supposed, be beating its wings now against the window-panes of his eyes – seeking the light outside since the inner radiance was already extinguished.

Gerald opened and closed his mouth, worked his gaze and his jaw and then jerked his head in the direction of the television set. Oh yes, of course, his favourite: *Top of the Pops*.

Walter came back at dusk when Tinker and Humph had heaved the house into some kind of shape. The beds were made, a fire was burning in the hearth, the twins were asleep, Jason and Penny were watching television, Molly had put up some curtains in the main room at least, Tess had made spaghetti and Gladys had helped.

It was Gladys who had sensed the presence of her adored Walter before, surely, anyone could have heard his step on the gravel, and let him in. Molly had meant to be angry but Walter, as ever, deflected wrath simply by being so Walter. His (spurious) expression of hunger, his damp tennis shoes, other-worldly smile, raggedy jacket, air of a tentative visitor even in his own house disarmed as they always did. Gladys would have wagged her tail if she had had one.

Walter hung up his jacket, sat down at the table and seemed not to notice the spaghetti Tess had put before him. He crumbled a little bread (very carefully – it might have been the Host), delivered it to his mouth, chewed it then swallowed some wine. If everyone was watching, he was oblivious of the fact.

'I've bought a boat,' he said.

Molly put down her fork. She closed her mouth, not to say but we can't afford a boat. Penny rolled her eyes.

Tinker grinned. 'Great. What sort of a boat, Pops?'

Walter smiled. He appeared very pleased with himself.

'Bit of a wreck, actually. There's a sail.'

Molly took a deep breath. 'Walter, you don't know how to sail.'

'I expect I'll learn. We do live by the sea.'

'Oh yes. We live by the sea.'

In bed Molly lay awake. She was aware of Walter breathing steadily beside her. She wished she could turn to him and say she was happy about the boat. She wished she could understand why she was not happy about the boat. And what had happened to her when the plate was dropped and smashed, or the moment before it broke, and what had been the meaning of her sea-dream last night and why she was afraid to sleep now, for fear of dreams.

Downstairs Penny was watching Rainer Werner Fassbinder's *Despair*. As the images flicked before her she nodded. She didn't know about reparations or any of that old history but it struck her as true in some sense she couldn't be bothered to analyse. She liked the bit about the wolves being invisible behind their howls. And Dirk Bogarde was terrific.

She watched with her mouth slightly open, plucking absently at the hard dead skin on her heels. When the film finished the late-night news came up and she shifted onto her stomach and turned off the sound. It looked like London, another riot, or it could have been Paris, or anywhere. There were people with crosses and people with stones and the pigs with their riot shields and helmets and clubs. She yawned and went to look for something to eat. There wasn't much so she settled for baked beans cold from the tin. She thought about the Fassbinder. It was like a dream and yet it was more real than the news. She wondered why people couldn't understand him. It was all quite obvious to her.

On the moors above, something wild barked. The sea with its load of creatures turned over and snatched another millimetre of the land it had once possessed, probed for more in crevices, seeking out the vulnerable passages, fingering for the frangible shale, the soft hidden entries to this coast of castellated granite.

There was always a sense of fantasy here, in this dream-country; or rather, of reality undermined, assumptions put in doubt, messages scrambled. Tenuously linked to England, this might have been an off shore island. It was something to do with the light and with age and a mumble of myth, secrets. Whatever it was drew Walter into deep sea-dreams and kept Molly awake.

All this could have been an imagining of Martha Price's or a dream of the Principessa's in the Channel Hotel. If there were a director. If there were a director at all there was no reason to suppose that he might be merciful.

Walter was thrashing in his sleep. Something had alarmed him. Molly propped herself on an elbow.

'Love. Wake up.'

'What?'

'A nightmare. That's all.'

'Oh. Yes.'

Walter rubbed his eyes.

Molly said: 'Would you like some tea?'

'I'll get it.'

She was almost asleep again by the time Walter came back. The tea was black and nearly cold and dark leaves floated on the surface.

'I couldn't find tea bags.'

'Doesn't matter.'

He looked penitent. He sat cross-legged on the bed, his tea untouched.

'D'you mind about the boat? I should have asked.'

'I did. A bit. I don't know why. Of course you must have a boat.'

'I could sell it again?'

He really meant it. His expression was so grave and anxious, it reminded her of Jason when he had broken something.

'No.' Molly put down her cup and took his hand. 'If you'll be careful. Now lie down.'

They did not make love but she traced his features with her finger and he kissed her face and then they clung together as desperately as though they were in danger and fell asleep like that, entwined.

FOUR

Molly had hoped for a family expedition to Poltrue but Walter announced he would make a solo crossing. So it was that while Gladys was left behind to mind the twins and harvest dandelions for Hazel, and Humph and Tinker to saw and plane and measure and sand, there was a parting at the quay. Walter strode off to his boat like a man to his bride. Molly, Tess, Penny and Jason took the ferry, pleased to be on the sea, which was flat and green as spring grass. Though when Molly peered closer, marvelling at the wonderful clearness, she thought she could discern a kind of muscular movement beneath the stretched surface, a pull in various contradictory directions.

Still, from the quay on the other side the skin of the water shone and smiled and while over the harbour all but their own house was in granite darkness, here there were people moving around in the light, fishermen landing their catch, a van drawn up to receive it, a man on a bench throwing a stick for a sheepdog that caught it in mid-air and brought it back to be thrown again, three women with shopping bags and one with a push-chair making their way down the steps to take the ferry back, a girl perched on the harbour wall, swinging a leg, one hand on a pram that held a sleeping baby, a boy leaning over the rail to shout to the fishermen who knew him and abused him back, a restaurant with blinds down and men at work painting, closed shutters on another of the low quayside buildings announcing hot pasties and pizzas, hunched youths smoking on the steps of the pub, rolling tobacco in thin paper, lounging, cracking elbows and letting out sudden sharp barks of canine laughter.

And there, three narrow disappearing streets leading up to town and church and shops. And Molly looked around her and thought, but this must be safe. Whatever could happen in a place like this?

'I'm sorry?'

Tess was saying which street should they take?

'I shouldn't think it matters. They probably all lead to the same place in the end.'

Molly found herself reluctant to leave the quay and blinked, blinded for a moment from the light of the quay as they entered a maze of stone steps and arches and shops and narrow, high walls and emerged at last in the cobbled main street where there was nothing after all more alarming than a Spar grocer, a fishmonger, two souvenir shops (closed), a chemist, a dress-shop, a window of antiques and the Treasure Chest displaying the remnants of last year's cheap and cheerful beads, Indian and Hong Kong cottons and hook-on plastic earrings.

Penny had wandered off on her own. Tess frowned at her list and said: 'I'll do the grocer. You look for fish.'

The fish-shop was on the dark side of the street, the window arranged like a child's picture, green rows of artificial parsley and in between the eyeless flatfish and dull gaze of mackerel and trout. A giant salmon, crustaceans Molly did not recognise and prime prawns all in a row. Jason pulled at her hand, drawn by the interior where in a miniature aquarium a single sole (so much larger than on the slab) circled in glum majesty, blubber-lips and flat eyes. At the front of the short queue a thin, sallow-faced woman in a dun-coloured cloak asked for eel. 'Smoked,' she said and the fishmonger in his blue-striped apron drew out from a pack of ice beneath the counter a serpent – or so it seemed; something wicked anyway. Molly saw him lift the cleaver and heard the crack as the spine broke. At that moment the woman turned and in her gaze Molly detected something: amusement? recognition?

The fishmonger had curls of black hair on the back of his hands and wore a straw boater, though at an angle that implied mockery – of himself or of his role.

'Well, my love, and what can we do for you?' He still held the cleaver and was wiping it with kitchen paper.

'Eel, I think,' Molly heard herself say, and shuddered.

'Granny's bought a snake for supper,' Jason told Tess, who raised her eyebrows.

Penny was sitting on a bollard on the quay.

'Pops is going out.'

'Oh dear, he's never sailed alone before.'

'Well, he's managing all right. Look.'

They looked. A light breeze had come up and there indeed, leaving the traffic of the harbour behind it, diminishing, no bigger already than a dark moth clinging precariously to the surface of the water, was a small craft with single full sail, carrying Walter out to sea.

From her seat beneath the eucalyptus in the garden of the Channel Hotel Norah Carteret watched Walter's progress and smiled, reminded of the soul as a moth escaping the bone-caged corpse, while on the Poltreth headland the stern black dog Enoch saw too and faintly growled. For Martha's Pounce spying for birds from the shelter of the early camellia, the sea was of no interest, except for the fish that came out of it.

It was not so difficult after all, Walter decided shifting his weight as the sea shouldered his boat over the swell, riding a movement that threatened yet never quite broke as a wave. He knew what to do next almost as though someone were guiding his hand. The wash of an incoming launch nearly heaved him over but the little boat corrected herself and outside the harbour a fresher breeze filled the sail and raised the bows so that for a wild moment she shuddered. Walter felt the tug, eased the sheet and settled back, the sun on his face, a light hand on the tiller. Before him were miles of kindly ocean, at his back, receding ever further, the land, the small grey cottages with their plumes of smoke, all the people on the land, England, the past, history, all he had lost, longed for, every trouble, hope, small pains; himself even. So this was the sea! Walter smiled. He began to sing.

'How do you cook eel?'

'You should have got it skinned.'

Waiting for the ferry, addressing Tess, who did not hear her, Molly jumped. There was the woman again, the one in the cloak.

'Terrible beast you are.'

While Molly and Tess lingered on the quay, waiting for Penny, Martha Price watched Pounce gulp the eel, hardly pausing to chew. Finished, the little cat gave one last swallow, shook his whiskers and, settled in a patch of sun, began to groom himself, purring faintly and tugging at his fur.

'That's enough,' said Martha. 'Work to do!'

'There's cloud coming in from the west. I do hope Walter will be all right.'

Back at Poltreth, Molly shivered. Why had she not noticed before how cold it was? Wherever had Gladys got to? Why had she bought eel? How did you cook it? Suddenly tired, she dumped her shopping and sat in the chair by the empty grate.

'How do you cook eel?'

Tess had already put on the kettle for coffee. Now she peeled open the newspaper parcel.

'Is it skinned? Oh yes. Well, you can fry it or do it *en matelote*. Only for that you need wine, pickling onions and button mushrooms.'

'We haven't got any,' said Molly faintly. Quite sharply, as though the thought had always been living like a toad in her mind, she resented Tess. Tess would know about eels. Tess knew everything. What would happen if one were to pull Tess's plait – hard?

Ashamed, Molly collected herself.

'It was silly. I don't know why I bought it.'

'It's all right anyway. It's smoked.'

'What do we do then?'

'Eat it as it is.'

'Raw?'

'With lemon. And brown bread and butter.'

'Oh yes. Of course.'

Molly was puzzled by her lethargy. It was natural she should have been exhausted yesterday but she had slept well. Yet her limbs were heavy and her eyes burned. Somewhere she could hear Humph and Tinker sawing.

'Gladys shouldn't have left the twins.'

'That's all right. Humph's around.'

Molly must have dozed because she woke suddenly as if someone had called.

On the cliffs Enoch growled.

Gladys picking dandelions, had Hazel on a lead.

'Hush, silly dog. It's only a pussy. Look, it's got a red collar. Come on, puss.'

The little black cat rubbed its spine against Gladys's ankles. Now they had a dog, Gladys thought, it would be nice to have a cat. She liked animals better than people, really. With people she always felt more alone than she was when by herself. That is, she had this feeling that she must be the person they expected her to be: dull and good. Oh, Tinker was a kind boy, he teased her and pretended she was a wild one, called her my beautiful Glad and she played along and blushed and let him hug her and peck her on the cheek. But the truth was, it was just pretending again because he wanted her to be pleased and she'd known and loved him since he was a scrap in nappies. She loved Walter too and when he remembered he was nice to her. But she knew quite well he would never notice if she turned into a hen, provided she laid well and he had clean socks. Perhaps not then. He never set much account by clothes or food and if no one bothered he'd do without both and just walk around with his soul showing.

Mind you, perhaps it was the sea air but since they came to Poltreth she'd had a funny feeling that something was changing: there was a new person inside her who might suddenly speak up or act quite differently. It could just be the old one getting out at last. Either way, it was a bit bothering but exciting too as if she'd suddenly found she could fly. That would make them all jump if old Glad sprouted wings and flapped her way over to Poltrue. That would make them think.

'Can you see Walter?' Molly came out of the cottage pushing her hands through her hair, trying to wake up properly. 'Is that him? Such a long way out. I wish he wouldn't. He doesn't know the sea. Has he turned? I can't tell.'

The dog Enoch gave a throaty whimper. He had taken station on the very edge of the cliff and seemed, like Molly, to be anxiously scanning the sea. The wind had changed (was that why she had woken?) and arguing with the ebb tide, created a humpy sea in which the craft that might be Walter's bucked alarmingly and sometimes was lost altogether. Perhaps it wasn't a boat at all but a wave?

Driven back by the wind, Molly gasped. How could Gladys go on picking dandelion leaves? Suddenly she would have liked to creep up behind Gladys and heave her over the cliff.

'Why is that cat watching us?'

'Cats do that. They're particular.'

I must not be sharp with Gladys.

'What do you mean, Gladys?'

'It's deciding about us. If it wants to stay.'

'We seem to have a dog already. We don't want a cat. Anyway, it must belong to someone. It has a collar.'

Molly and Gladys looked at Pounce in his smart red flea collar. Pounce looked back at them, arched his back to yawn and high-stepped towards the cottage. Enoch appeared oddly wary of the small animal and made no attempt to intervene as Pounce inspected the water-butt, the messy yard, sniffed a potted geranium and after a judicious pause at the back door, considered entering the cottage but changed his mind. Perhaps he was put off by the man-smell or the sound of Humph and Tinker sawing or he may simply have seen enough for the moment.

Molly laughed a little shakily at his antics.

'Puss?' She crouched. 'Puss, come here. Come on.'

The little cat advanced, permitted Molly to scratch his chin, offered his flank and spine, purred faintly, then was off. Molly wondered whyever she felt so cold.

'Well, that's cats for you, isn't it. We needn't have worried. He belongs to someone.' For a second she had forgotten Walter. The wind was freshening alarmingly now. Hazel looked thankful to be back in her cage. 'Walter. Where is he? I can't see him at all now. Can you see him?'

Heading back reluctantly towards the land, Walter had noticed the wind change but not the squall at his back. He let the sail fill and the boat run but this time she bucked uncomfortably. The sea made no sense. It lulled him, allowing a gentle ride up and down the other side of an alarming-looking hill, then a small mean wave would come from nowhere, slap the boat about and empty itself in the cockpit.

Barely in control of a boat so much smaller than the hounding seas, without a bailer and with wet feet, it was astonishing how desirable appeared the land he had left so joyfully. From here he could see his own home, the coastguard cottage, figures at the cliff-edge (Molly? And that might be Gladys?). Then he fell into a trough and it was as if they, not he, had sunk.

Flung beam-on to the seas, Walter saw the darkness rolling in behind him and his mood changed. Matters were taken from his hands. No cliff. No Enoch. Simply the chaos of the ocean. To give way. To drown. To die. Not so much really. It was life that was perilous and fragile, fearful. Easy to go like this, let go.

Then as suddenly as the wind had changed, it fell light. The scene was sunny and cheerful. There was the ferry, a wind-surfer out of wind lolling on his board. Land sounds: a dog barking (Enoch?), children calling from the small beach, the church clock at Poltrue.

On her terrace Martha Price fed her datura – that plant of yellow flower and poison – and from the window of the small greenhouse nodded as the squall slipped off to the east, leaving behind a blameless sky of such innocence it might never have heard of tempest. To the east that day a fishing boat sank and by the time the squall had finished its affairs there were two widows made. Orphans too.

Martha looked again. Now Walter was becalmed, drifting backwards in fact, and crabwise. Well, that would do him no harm for a bit. Let him row against the current and learn that the sea is female. Forgives nothing.

Ah, now he was in the Poltrue whirlpool, that secret confusion discernible only on the calmest day. The water at its deepest. There had been drownings.

Martha watched. Leave him there? No. Naughty. She took off her gardening gloves, walked to the edge of her terrace and reached out a hand.

'We meet again.'

The feeling Walter had was not so much that the whirlpool had let him go. Rather, he had the sensation of being plucked from the waters. One moment he was spinning round in alarming circles, the next he was sitting in the sun on this woman's terrace, with a generous glass in his hand.

'Home brew. Hope that's all right.'

'I'm sure,' said Walter. He looked at his drink. It was the colour of pale straw, nearly opaque, but the scent was subtle, flowery. He took a sip. 'Mmn.' Then another. The woman was watching him. 'Very good.'

'I'm Martha Price.'

'Walter Waterman.'

'I know.'

'The current. Down there. Extraordinary.'

'That's what Poltrue means – whirlpool.'

'I'll remember that next time.' Walter normally regarded strangers with the caution most would reserve for aliens or mad dogs. He rarely asked people about themselves in case they told him but he felt more at ease than usual. Perhaps the sea, in spite of its tempers, was good for the nerves. 'Are you a native then?'

She shook her head. It was quite a relief to find that it was not pointed. What age could she be, he wondered? Anything from thirty five to fifty.

'Not exactly. I've lived here on and off a long time.'

'No family?' Walter was thinking of a husband, a man, a son even. That is to say, he was not exactly thinking such unWalterish thoughts any more than he was observing that the top button of Martha Price's shirt was undone to the point where one could just see the cleft between her breasts. She was very brown or perhaps she was normally pigmented that interesting shade of tan.

Interesting? Molly was the only woman he had ever found interesting. And lately he had grown not disloyal but just a shade detached. When they made love he had seen himself once or twice sitting somewhere up in the corner where ceiling met wall, watching himself make love. It struck him with the surprise of which only innocence is capable, that he was not a very good husband.

'No,' Martha said. 'Not what you'd call family. Just a couple of sisters. We telephone. But the wind's come up again. Let's go indoors.'

Walter was not a man who noticed houses.

He was aware of a feeling of well-being, that was all. Vaguely, his consciousness took in the fact that the room was unusually large. Tall, that was it: must have knocked out a floor to achieve such height. From the outside the house had looked no more than a cottage. Within, purblind from the sun, he could hardly make out where the ever-climbing walls met the pointy ceiling. Almost like a church. A spiral staircase led down, presumably to lower floors. Rooms? Cellars?

Walter would be the first to admit that he had no idea what a home should be. Molly made homes. They were Molly-places and all had a certain smell and texture to which he was accustomed. All he asked was that things stay where they were. The slightest change and he would bark his shins. When the children were small he had tripped on Tinker's articulated snake and though it was his ankle he sprained it was his back that twinged in wet weather, even to this day. First, they put a board in the bed. Then he tried sleeping on a mat on the floor and would never have returned to the bed, given a free choice.

Walter blinked. What was the woman saying?

Martha had brought in a saucer from the terrace and was rinsing it under a tap in what appeared to be a kitchen area. Yes, a kitchen, definitely. As Walter grew accustomed to the shadows, the spare furnishings of the room took shape: cooker, sink, sleeping gallery, divan, trestle table. But there was so little on the floor the eye was drawn upwards to that high dimness where there was nothing.

'I'm sorry?'

'Eel, I said.' Her movements were neat, quick, deft. She had very long, dark hair tied at the back. 'My cat. The Celts used to burn them, you know. They thought they were witches.'

'Cats?'

'Serpents. And cats. Do you fish?'

'Not yet. I suppose I should.'

She refilled his drink then poured one for herself, lit a cigarette and sat down in the straight-backed chair facing Walter. For a thin woman her breasts were large. As she bent over his glass he smelled their warmth.

'Why should you fish?'

'I don't know. I don't know why I said that.'

'There's been a change, you know.'

Change?

'Something to do with the Humboldt Current. The North Atlantic drift. Portuguese men-o '-war. Turtles. Sharks. Flying fish. Reports of a sea-snake.'

Walter had the most extraordinary impulse to put his nose between those breasts and snuff. There was a smell of fish in the air rising from whatever went on at the foot of the spiral staircase.

'Just the rest of the eel cooking. I've got a range down there and a smoker.' Martha smiled: a glimpse of small, sharp teeth, a little discoloured. 'You can do wonders with lemon and a few herbs.'

Cooking was not Walter's domain. Molly always said you could feed him grass and he wouldn't notice.

'When I was a child I once lived on grass for a week.'

Walter glanced round, startled at the sound of his own voice. He was not one for confessions. Strangers he let slip by at shoulder-level beneath his lankiness. He had been known to cross the road to avoid acquaintances. He sometimes wondered however he had got himself married.

'Why did you do that?'

Walter blushed.

'To see if I could. I was trying to be good, I think.' Holy, he meant. The time of vocation. When the others masturbated he woke every morning in the hope of finding upon his hands and feet the miraculous stigmata. He even cut his own palms with a penknife and walked around for a week with his fists clenched in his pockets. The knife had been dirty and the wounds were very painful. He was young though. They healed and he gave up the Imitatio. The possibility of blasphemy padded after him all that term.

Bedwetter Waterman. Walter the wetter. Walter Waters.

'You believe in goodness?' she asked.

At the word, Martha had paused, lighter in one hand, cigarette in the other, alert. What's in this drink? thought Walter. He was grateful to be in shadow.

'I think,' he said, 'I believe against all evidence one must hope. Be ready. Look out for the opportunity? And you?'

Martha stood, stalked her room from one ashtray to another, spilling grey flakes.

'I believe in power. Powers. Neither good nor evil. Neutral. Depends how you use them. If you use them. Most people don't.'

Did she? Walter wondered for an insane second. Then he returned to his senses.

'You mean like priests.'

Walter had never met anyone who listened so intently. Well, Molly listened, of course, but she had a Molly kind of way of doing something else at the same time. Since the children, anyway. That is, she had developed the habit when the children were small, and still, whenever she was addressed at what promised to be any length, she reached at once for knitting, beans to be sliced, in the same way she watched television. Walter had never thought of it before but it did pass through his mind now as he saw the Martha Price person dip her head in single-minded consideration of his question, that most women who had men and children and, often, jobs, must lead lives of a complexity that appalled him. That would have appalled him if he had allowed himself to dwell on it. As it was, Martha Price had finished digesting his feeble answer and snapped her head up.

'Priests? Yes, under certain circumstances. They truly flourish only where there is poverty, ignorance and envy. The Ayatollahs are like the ancient sorcerers, the medieval church-men or the Catholic Church today in some parts. The Maleficium was impotent without the conspiracy of society. If you didn't believe, you were untouchable. White magic worked the same way. Still does. Poetry too. You need the connivance of the reader, the openness to belief. With any writing, I suppose.'

It suddenly struck him.

'Are you a writer?'

Thank God, the woman had sat down, ceased her stalking. She stretched, scattering ash again. She smiled her weird smile, which turned down the corners of her mouth.

'You could say I write. Or I did write. Not the same thing.'

'May I ask what?'

'Novels. A novel. And before you ask, it was neither romance nor thriller.' She ground out her stub and fiddled for another cigarette. 'I'm sorry. That was rude of me. It's just what most people assume. Most men. But you're not most men, are you?' That glinting attention then and a wider smile.

'Are you writing anything now?'

'Researching. That's a good way of putting off writing. It could be forever. You are different, aren't you? Open?'

'My wife paints,' Walter offered, as though to summon Molly. Or rather, what he thought of as Molly-sense, the way she could always be counted on. Not a matter to which he normally gave much thought.

'I know. I'd like to meet her. I'm thinking of starting a small group.'

'Writing?'

'Oh, this and that. To tell you the truth, I've been at a bit of a loose end lately. Women are in this place unless they play bridge and then they go mad. It's all right for the men. They sail. And when they can't sail any more they die. They die first, anyway. This is widow-land.' Martha reflected. 'This is a terrible place, you know. Don't be misled by all that Flurry Dance stuff.

The Celts are still strong here and they are a violent people. Incest. Suicide. Rape. Anyway, I'll get in touch with your wife.'

'I'm sure she'd like that,' Walter said, not sure at all.

'Well, we'll see.'

Martha had startled herself a little. Perhaps she had been lonely. Alone, anyway. Suddenly the idea of breaking the mould of her solitariness seemed attractive. Provided, of course, she controlled the circumstances and the outcome.

She walked with Walter to the terrace. The wind had dropped and the sun was high and hot.

'We'll meet again.'

'I hope so.'

'Oh, we shall.'

Martha watched him start down the steps.

'You'll have to row over. Be careful.'

Walter waved thank you. He clutched the handrail and looked back and up at Martha on her terrace in the bright sun. She raised a hand in salute and he felt sure he was mistaken. It must be that drink. Or his eyes, coming from the darkness into the light, but just for a second he could have sworn that Martha Price had no shadow.

As Walter rowed across to Poltreth, the ferry was returning to Poltrue. This early in the season there were few passengers: a couple of non-smoking, teetotal, vegetarian ramblers making the crossing to resume their cliff walk, exclaimed at the sight of the small, black cat with the red collar that had nipped aboard at Poltreth and even before the ferryman had thrown a warp round the bollard jumped, sure-footed, ashore at Poltrue.

Less steady on his feet, Walter landed. His back gave warning as he struggled to haul the boat up the beach. Two tall Cornishmen with strong arms and black beards and one Celtic gnome in a knitted hat that looked as if it had been screwed into his head, watched Walter's efforts with professional interest. They shook their heads sympathetically as he finally heaved his craft above the high-water mark. For a moment he collapsed on his knees, one hand to his complaining spine. He gasped to catch his breath and the dwarf turned to his companion.

'He'll need a mooring for that, then.'

The other studied Walter.

'He'll not get one.'

At least Enoch was waiting for him. That was something. A brief half-wag of greeting, a sniff of Walter's hand, and the black dog led Walter up the hill, walking a little ahead, turning every so often to make sure his master followed.

As Walter plodded home, oars over his shoulder, he wondered what the Martha Price woman had meant. She was certainly right about one thing: he was not, alas, most men. He sat outside the bright window of life, amazed by the busy passions beyond his experience. The Anglo-Saxons had a word for it: *mondream* – the dream of life among men.

But then, open, she had said. He was open.

Empty was the word Walter himself would have used, but then perhaps it amounted to the same thing – a void, a vessel. Something that can be filled? Certainly since the end of the Earthfolk he had been aware of a lack of purpose. Then, coming here, a change. Sea-change? A feeling, at least, that alteration was possible. Catching his breath at the cliff-top, he looked out to sea. The squall had quite blown out. There was a skein on the water now, like a net, upon which rode a fishing boat; further out, a small, white triangle of a sail had been pinned to the horizon – a yacht heading west. Walter felt suddenly vertiginous at the thought of those vast waters: heaving, ebbing and flooding as the moon ordained, all on the spinning planet.

He shook his head, wondering again what the woman had put in that drink, then there was Gladys waving and Molly, a step behind her, calling.

Tinker said: 'Did you know the body is three-quarters water? Hey, Glad, what's this? Worm? You might have cooked it.'

'Eel,' Molly said. 'Smoked. Squeeze some lemon on it. And here's the pepper.'

'Where d'you catch it, Ma?'

'I bought it. I'm sorry, I'm not used to seafood.'

'It's fine. Why aren't you eating it?'

Molly pushed her plate aside and managed not to shudder. 'Just not hungry, that's all.'

'What a pity,' said Gladys. 'There's some nice junket?'

'I'm rather tired. I think I'll go to bed.'

She was still awake when Walter came up to bed.

'All right?'

'Fine.' Well, one had to be fine with Walter. He had a horror of other people's infirmities. When Tinker was born he was in India with Mother Teresa. The day of Penny's arrival he was saving seals (in fact, Molly had half suspected he would have preferred Penny to be a seal). Fortunately, Molly was strong. Her only fall from grace had been in the plague winter of Asian flu (was that really nearly thirty years ago?). She had been touched then almost beyond bearing by the fact that Walter had actually entered her sickroom. Or, rather, inserted his head round the door wearing the expression of an anxious heron. Dimly, from the deep seas of her fever, Molly had grasped what this gesture meant. He was checking up to make sure she was not dying. Because he loved her? Or because he needed her, in the world, to be left often but to be there upon his return to Ithaca?

And what if one day she were to break her loom, take the suitors to her breast? Unthinkable, of course, as unlikely as that he would linger in some Circe's arms. Not that there hadn't been candidates. Women had regarded Walter's innocence as a rich prize, failed to capture the booty simply because he wore that very innocence, unknowing, as a shield. They looked greedily at him and he, divinely protected, looked past them.

Stooping to undress under the low ceiling, he groaned.

'Your back?'

'Mmn.'

'Come here. Let me. That's right, turn over.' She knew the places, how to give him ease: the base of the neck then the lumbar region around the spine. When Walter slipped on Tinker's articulated snake the osteopath said there was a lot of lumbar distress around nowadays. As though Walter had gone seeking a serpent upon which to dislocate himself.

'Are you sure that boat isn't too much for you?'

Molly paused in her knuckling. Walter slept, a sea-dream green and deep.

Now it was dark, the Principessa woke in the Ocean Suite of the Channel Hotel. Her drug-dreams had been thick. Tomorrow she might call them to wheel her into the gardens. Born Annie Stubbs, she had been the star Nancy Forrest and it was Nancy who made up her face, knew all the Hollywood tricks.

The Principessa slipped on her cowled wrap and her rings and walked the empty passages of the hotel. She had bird bones and walked with arms outstretched, fingers splayed to feel the air before her. In the ballroom Nancy danced to her secret saxophone.

Awake in bed beside Gerald, Norah Carteret sighed with satisfaction and laid down her Anita Brookner. That calm style – old-fashioned nowadays, she supposed. So many frantic writers, poor souls. Why did they have to shout so? Not that those sad Brookner gels were exactly cheering but one always knew what they wore (that dreadful cardigan – poor Edith Hope!). All they needed was a change of wardrobe. Norah herself had always found a new frock very helpful.

Novels were a great comfort, not to be taken in place of life but worlds, at least, in which she could wander by herself. Rather like going to a party where you might meet someone new and wonderful. Which reminded her of that nice Mrs Waterman. She must find a pretext to see her again.

Miss Brookner slipped from Norah's hand. Not that she ever slept deeply. Her mental alarm woke her every hour all through the night. Then she would watch Gerald's shoulders to make sure he still breathed.

My name is Fenny Trevanion and I am mumble-jumble. I scares children for the wart on my nose and my poor cloths and my good black dog, my best boy, they runs from he and would hurt he if they can but he runs faster. So we keep to ourselves and we are fine enough in our hut. (Testimony

taken by the clerk, Richard Rashlay at the witch-trial of Fenny
Trevanion, Launceston, 1648.)

In her house on the highest point of the cliff, Martha was trying
to work. She found it unusually hard to concentrate. That man
from the water had cracked the shell of her solitude. She put
aside Fenny Trevanion, stretched, and took a book from the
heap on her butcher's block desk, opened at random and read.

'Characteristics of witches: such women are frequently iso-
lated and depressed. They may carry snakes in their bellies.
They work in secret at night. Calamities attributable to malice
of witches: plague, drought, death, sickness, storm. Practices:
Incest. Bestiality. Cannibalism against their own children.'

Martha snorted. That fool Midwinter, what did he know?
Midwinter, who should know everything, understood nothing.
But then what did any man know of a power you never asked
to be born with? I am a woman who has had a hysterectomy,
living alone, and I cannot weep. I hear more than I can bear –
the keening of the bright widows at their bridge, the death-croak
of a child in Ethiopia. Oh yes, I know, put me on trial for the
sea-widows I made today. But remember the sadness of
witches. No wonder they are tempted by tricks – think, for a
moment, what it is to be shut out from the warm rooms of life.
Perhaps you too feel it sometimes? Anyone who has walked the
cliffs alone and seen spring lovers twined in the hollows. Who
has stood outside on a dark night, watched the talking within,
the laughing, the touching, the flesh against flesh, and had the
curtain drawn against them and gone home alone. You? You?

Martha went to the terrace door. 'Pounce?'

Gone tomming, damn cat.

She gazed beyond the lights of Poltrover, out to sea. Shivered
at the thought that hung in the corner of her mind like a bat.
Something beneath the waters. The deep worm?

Martha slammed the door behind her. Let the little beast use
the cat flap.

Perhaps just tonight a whisky. Or two. Bed. Bottle. Glass.
Fags. She climbed to the sleeping gallery, stripped, lay down,
poured a drink.

Ring Morwena and Judith, she wondered? Who could you talk
to if not your own sisters? She closed her eyes and could see
Judith in Australia, the pretty girl in her bright morning kitchen,
the kettle on the hob, big marmalade Ringer purring by the
stove. Judith barefoot in her old Laura Ashley print, plaiting her
mass of golden hair, cultivating her sunflowers, humming among
her herbs.

No. Judith would fuss. Morwena in Connecticut? Martha
dialled.

'Martha? Do you know what the hell time it is here?'

'You weren't asleep.'

'Just a few of the girls in. Martha, when are you coming over?
You can really feel at home here. I've no patience with you.'

Martha grinned.

'I know. You've told me.'

'Don't you *want* to come out of the closet?'

'Not particularly.'

'Have you been drinking?'

'A bit.'

'Martha, listen to me. You're alone too much with your malice.
I've got to go now – the girls are waiting – but I want you
seriously to consider coming over. We have a really fine shrink.
One of us.'

'No thanks, Morwena. Good night.'

'Martha, don't cut me off. Martha –'

Martha put down the receiver and pulled out the wall-plug.
She drained her whisky, picked the area around her toes for dry
skin, eased herself onto the other elbow. She had already
forgotten why she had wanted to talk to Morwena. She lay back,
ran her fingers through her bush and over the belly that would
never bear child. Her breasts felt heavy tonight. She touched
herself like a lover but there was something despondent, unutterably lonely about the warm shudder when it came.

Dreams met and mingled and soared above the waters between
Poltreth and Poltrue like the assembly of gulls at their mysteri-
ous, mute, sunset gathering. In the Poltrue Cottage Hospital a
life went out gently with the ebb-tide and at the same moment

the sac of amniotic waters broke in the belly of an unwed daughter of Poltreth. Martha saw all this. Saw too much. Knew that the child swimming to birth would perish on the first day of the last war at an ancient crossroads in Palestine. The other soul she accompanied a little way before turning back. The fat moon showed her a glitter on the sea bed that could be scales. She flicked up the Nile from Cairo to Aswan, where on Elephantine Island feathers were nailed to a door. In Giza a barren woman tended a brown fowl whose blood in the morning would break the hex upon her. Martha could have gone further, seen all from the first to the last.

At times when her malice had been upon her she had spied upon the end of everything and even now she saw the locusts gathering in Africa but, riding her dream, turned away. In her younger days when she rode with Morwena, what glee she would have from calling up a sandstorm, tidal wave! The extent of her powers she had never truly tested and, growing fearful of her spite, all but put away her tricks.

At four in the morning, the dying time, Molly felt herself jerked awake. Something at the window? Must have been a dream. All the same she would do something about curtains. Tomorrow. Meanwhile she curled closer to Walter.

Dawn found Martha Price sleeping, a shawl from Aleppo flung over her lower limbs, Pounce curled at her breast like a suckling child.

FIVE

Something is going to happen, Martha thought, and it could be my fault.

Don't brood. Get on with the ordinary things. Morwena was right. I am alone too much. I shall alter that.

So Martha reflected, standing on her terrace in the morning light. Bright before seven, rain by eleven. She tugged at the rock samphire that had invaded her wall and attacked the stone but she liked the sour-sweet smell.

She sniffed her fingers, pulled her shawl around her and settled with her coffee in the lounger, closed her eyes. When she opened them, there, on the Poltreth headland was a child on a swing, silhouetted against the sky. Each time it extended its reach it looked as though it might fly off and away. At the highest point of the arc (very high – a daring child, clearly) Martha was tempted to pluck it off and let it fall or fly.

Yes, she did feel better this morning. Last night's mood had cleared as mysteriously as it had arrived. It was a fine day. She had health and strength, powers and knowledge. Self-pity was not becoming to her kind, she should take pleasure in her gifts. A spot of mischief? Why not?

Which reminded her.

Martha went indoors to her desk, pushed aside the Fenny Trevanion file, took down the Bible from her shelf. It had clearly been opened many times at the same page. Although she knew it already by heart, Martha read, inhaling greedily from her cigarette and letting the ash fall:

And I heard a great voice out of the temple saying to the seven angels, Go your ways and pour out the vials of the wrath of God upon the earth.

And the first went, and poured out his vial upon the earth; and there fell a noisome and grievous sore upon the men which had the mark of the beast, and upon them which worshipped his image.

And the second angel poured out his vial upon the sea; and it became as the blood of a dead man: and every living soul died in the sea.

Martha nodded, her eye flicking over the rest. Then she reached for the key on the fine silver chain from around her neck and unlocked a shallow drawer that at first sight would have been taken for a part of the frame. From a bulging wallet file newspaper cuttings spilled.

'Pounce, shove off.'

The cat who had been perched on the beam above the desk landed on four paws in the middle of the cuttings. Martha pushed him gently and he leaped again, settling like a lopsided fur tippet on her shoulder. Martha idly shuffled the clippings. Break-out from AIDS quarantine camp. An old one that. Nuclear plant beneath Negev. Nerve gas at Sammara. Fishing banned North Sea. No-go areas Liverpool, Birmingham, Bristol. London threatened. SYRIA GOES NUKE.

Martha yawned. Idiot man could be trusted to get on with the inevitable process. He needed no helping hand from herself or the great I Am. What interested her were the so-called natural phenomena. Ah, this was better; EUPHRATES DRYING UP: Experts baffled. She could have told them, she who had glimpsed darkly the rough beast himself, shuffling towards Bethlehem, waiting to be born. Born long ago, brought to term and delivered of itself, she had seen it claw at its caul, bite through its own cord. Sniffed its pelt on the desert air. Rode it once for a mile or two until the stench was too much even for her. Known it well in many guises. Too well.

Oh yes, things are coming on, Pounce, you beast.

Quake in Connecticut. Morwena, do I detect your fine hand?

'Pounce, things seem to be speeding up. We'll need a bigger file.'

As so often when she had allowed herself the wicked pleasure of her secret drawer, Martha, putting away her file, returning to the world of her room (how drab, how dreary, how dark), felt a woe like winter rain. She shivered, crossed her arms across her breast, dipped her face to nuzzle Pounce's warm fur. Wished as a child for comfort, company.

As she had foreseen, the sun had gone, the sky leaked a mean grey. Pounce twitched the tip of his tail and struggled from too tight an embrace and Martha had not the heart to curse him.

What had Morwena said? Oh, yes.

Martha made a list and a number of telephone calls. The list was very short. There were of course those she knew of who doubtless knew her well enough. Dodgy, but if she were seriously planning to carry through her resolution she would have to take risks to bring up the numbers. It might be interesting in any case to discover how many of her own kind there really were (had the dairy-woman's wart deceived her?).

The penultimate call was to directory enquiries, the last the most important of all. Martha dared not admit to herself how much it mattered.

The telephone had been installed yesterday but this was the first time it had rung. Molly jumped, torn between answering it and keeping an eye on Jason. He was swinging much too high and already this morning's wink of sun had gone. It would rain soon. Where was Penny? How did Jason thrive so on neglect? Thank heaven, the swing was slowing down.

'Oh yes, of course. In the fishmonger's. And you've met my husband? Thank you. I'm sure we'd love to come.'

'Love to what where?' said Penny, yawning, fresh from her bed. She picked at a piece of cold toast from the breakfast table, sighed, sank down on the sofa with the broken spring and, letting slip the duvet in which she was wrapped, took the twins to her breasts. She treats them like kittens, Molly thought. But then cats make good mothers.

'Oh, just an invitation.'

'I thought you had to be dead here before anyone spoke to you.'

'Well, you were wrong.'

'You're feeling better, aren't you?

'Yes, thank you. I am.'

Molly answered automatically. Her mind was elsewhere. What did people wear at parties nowadays? Whatever, she felt sure she didn't have it. Chopping onions towards the Allgoods' farewell supper, she ran mentally through her wardrobe. Most of it had been run up by Gladys, with a few things from the Oxfam shop. Years ago, she vaguely remembered she had tried, until it dawned upon her that Walter simply didn't see her. That is, he was aware of her presence only in the sense that he might notice her absence. He was tall, she was short, so far below his line of vision he had been known literally to overlook her, calling for her when she was there at his elbow. Oddly, it had never occurred to her to dress for herself. Tess would say she lacked self-image and maybe she did. Not that Tess could talk. She'd only ever seen her in trousers and Humph's cast-off sweaters. And there was something aggressive about the way Tess wouldn't wear make-up, as though virtue lay in a shiny nose. (Now there was a sharp thought – not the first to arrive unsummoned in Molly's mind since they came here.)

'Damn.' The knife slipped. Molly considered her finger. Blood. Interesting. Knives. Dark menstrual blood. In forty years how much did a woman bleed? A bathful? A pond? All the women in the world could treble the oceans, at least. Womb-blood, birth-blood, great red seas to drown small forked men. Were there men who didn't mind? Even in his prime, at the cottage, as corn-king, her lord of earth smelling of soil and abundance, Walter was shy of the blood-days.

'Ma!'

What was Penny saying?

'You've cut yourself. You're bleeding.'

'Oh dear, the onions.'

'Never mind the onions. Here, watch the twins, sit down, I'll get a plaster.'

Molly sucked her finger, waiting for Penny to come with the

plaster. The rain was slashing down now. Poltrue had been blotted out. Molly was wondering which was Martha Price's house. She felt an extraordinary peace and stillness, a given moment of wonder as the falling waters were whipped for a second aside to reveal a tremulous rainbow. Then the door crashed open and Jason, wet as a dog, flung himself against her skirt.

'Granny, I swinged, did you see me?'

Molly smiled. She buried her face in the boy's wet hair, the smell of him. For the pleasure of it. And to hide her tears.

At the club Norah was less aware of the rainbow than she might have been. When she handed in the key at the hotel desk on the way out there had been a small envelope now tucked into her handbag. While Gerald was drinking his pink gin – the one a day the doctor allowed – she had taken a quick peek. She sighed. It was out of the question, of course. Impossible to take Gerald. Impossible to leave him. Their party days were long over. Nice to be asked, all the same. Surprising too. While everyone knew everyone in Poltrue, she could remember speaking to the Price woman (Mrs or Miss? the note gave no clue) only once. She had come upon her gathering driftwood on the beach. Well, not so much a beach as a foreshore almost entirely covered at high water. The woman had cut an odd figure with her cloak, her basket and her little cat at her heels but when Norah spoke had been friendly enough, though not disposed to linger. Quite possibly she was lonely. This was no place for a young woman alone and Norah had noticed more than once how easy it is to slip by accident into a solitude that then becomes a habit hard to break.

That was one reason – apart from a cheap lunch – that Norah kept up with the club. A newcomer looking in would have seen a lot of old trouts (and so we are, Norah supposed). A roll-count from younger, happier days was depressing. But because we shared those days – we always came first to Gerald's mother then to the Channel Hotel on long leaves, we dreamed of it as home – we alone can see in each other our former selves. A stroke for the Colonel, replacement hip joint here, arthritis

everywhere; but how pretty Peggy had been, Duggy such a
dancer you'd never believe! Had it been true about him and
Mary Winstone? Who could say now? Mary long dead and Duggy
deaf as a post. You could hardly bawl such a question.

(Why post, Norah wondered, her mind flitting? Is it that rocks
can hear?)

So we grow old and sit at separate tables. Nice cloths nowadays and the new steward always puts a posy even if the chairs
are hard on bones from which the flesh has fallen. In summer
the young come through, sailing, and we can watch the races
from the terrace. Bamboo chairs in the bar. In the old days the
women came in through the back door but they have their own
powder-room now – not just loos but a mirror, properly lit and
a dressing-table for dinner nights.

Not a bad place to be beached.

Daphne Mount has just said was Norah coming to the Ladies
Dinner Club for once? Such an exciting speaker. Midwinter. You
know, the witch man? I'm not sure, Daphne, I'll have to see.
Gerald, you know . . . Thank the Lord sometimes for Gerald.
In Norah's opinion a gathering of women in evening dress was
as unnatural as a flight of hens. Had Daphne really said witch?

Norah cut up Gerald's mutton.

She passed the plate back, put the fork in Gerald's hand and
prayed that hand, fork and meat would manage to make the
perilous journey to his mouth. He found a spoon easier, she
knew, but just as she went on talking to him even without
response, it seemed vital that he should handle a fork as long
as he could. Would the time come when she had to feed him?
Wipe his face? Help him to the lavatory? Do other things for
him she preferred not to contemplate. Things she could not do
for a man with such a large frame. The young sailing doctor had
been breezily brutal. Best all round frankly if Gerald just pegged
out. Last stages could be long drawn out and difficult for everyone. Paralysis. Incontinence. No spring chicken yourself. Limit
to social services. While the manager of the Channel Hotel had
made it clear that his establishment was, you must understand
I fear, an hotel not a nursing home. If he were free, of course,
but the other residents and visitors.

Norah glanced at Gerald. The fork had delivered the gobbet of rather stringy mutton, the hand that had made the shaky passage to the mouth now trembled on the table-cloth and Norah was reminded sharply of last liver-Wednesday when it had struck her, as if a voice had spoken, that she disliked her husband. The busyness of the years, the great heap of the past had piled up so that she could not imagine living without him. And yet. Norah shook her head. There were questions better not asked, for fear of the answers. And surely she had loved him? She had married him in love?

His mouth was working.

Norah snapped open the bag on her lap and let her hand rest for a second on the folded paper. Would it be thinkable, possible even, to strike out in a small way on her own?

'You see, Gerald, all this time I was missing a sense of myself.'

Norah was hardly aware she had spoken aloud and in any case Gerald was involved in some great battle of his own. The throat strained. The hand made a slicing movement sideways.

'Puh,' he said.

'Yes, the mutton's not very good. The sprouts are quite crisp though. Here, give me your fork.'

While his mouth struggled to shape the word, Gerald shook his head, slicing still with his hand until he had all but knocked the plate from the table. Norah caught it just in time.

'Pudding,' he said. 'Damn sprouts. Pudding!'

'If you hadn't cut me off last night I'd have told you.' As dusk advanced on the west coast of England (twenty minutes later here than London), Martha woke from one of those terrible afternoon winter sleeps as deep as death and groped for the telephone. The room was thick with shadows while across the water in Poltreth merry lights burned.

'Martha? Are you still there?'

'What time it is?' Martha found the cigarettes but no matches.

'Midday here. What does it matter what time it is?'

Martha could see Morwena, the Autumn Beech-rinsed American matron snapping the head off a stick of celery, dipping a cracker in the cottage cheese. She could see her as she talked.

'Did you say Midwinter?' Ah, the matches. Where's the lamp? Martha pushed her hands through her hair. 'Why the hell would Midwinter be coming to Poltrue?'

'Nothing to do with you?'

Martha scowled. 'I'd hoped never to see him again.'

'Quite. Have you had his new book? *The Devil's Hand-maidens*?'

'An early copy. It's not on sale here yet.'

'Well, all I know is he was in Boston last week doing a signing session and he said he was flying straight over after Salem. He'll be in London, then a tour, then to that ghastly rock you live on. You've read the book?'

'Dipped in. Wanted to chuck it in the stove. All that stuff about pacts with Satan! He, of all people, knows that's not how we work. To perpetuate such rubbish –'

'Exactly.' Morwena was looking even keener than usual. Smug. She went on: 'And he can't be allowed to. The girls on the Anti-Defamation League here are hot to nail him.'

'Fat chance. He's still who he is. The great I Am.'

Morwena had one of those telephones you don't have to hold. While she talked she was doing her nails. Black.

'I'm not so sure, Martha. Times are changing. He's outnumbered by millions and everyone a libber. He may be a world authority on vampirism among the Azande but I'm damned if I'll have *him* badmouthing us. We have enough of a problem with those amateurs and their crazy orgies. This does matter, you know, Martha.'

'Does it?'

Morwena was wearing her red jump-suit. She was very much into her body, as she put it, and Martha had to admit that she looked good. Depressingly lithe and clear-eyed, so thin you might take her for a girl from the backside. The trouble with Morwena was that she had no sense of humour. Pointless to tease her.

Martha closed her eyes and the image of her sister faded. Not that that would stop her talking.

'Martha, you have to understand that we are coming into our time. Open any newspaper. Even the shrinks are jumping here

– better than the Wall Street crash. In a period of desperate insecurity it's the charismatic church or us. We haven't had it so good for 300 years. Which do you want? Those fat-cat preachers with pulpits in the White House or Witchpower?'

Martha thought of her bulging file of newspaper clippings.

'I'm not sure I really care, Morwena.'

'You're getting as bad as Judith,' Morwena snorted.

'Judith's happy.'

'Judith's a vegetable.'

'She's quite rich now.'

'White Witch Cucumber Face Creams! She's just a child, playing.'

Morwena sighed. 'So, what are you going to do about Midwinter coming? You're the one who had the fling with him.'

'Don't remind me.'

'You're on your own there. Be careful. He may have had his day at the top – well, who needs him now, just look at the world – but because he's sold out to the bestseller list doesn't mean he isn't dangerous. You haven't got a sisterhood behind you. You must think how you're going to handle him.'

'Maybe I'll ask him to a party,' Martha said. 'I'm going to hang up now, Morwena. Bye.'

Martha lay in the dark for a while. Well, who'd have thought of it – Midwinter in Poltrue. On and off through the years she had noted his progress. As a plague rat, a mullah in Iran, a green monkey in Africa, but he wasn't fit for much more than conjuring tricks nowadays. The world was going to hell without any help from him. Could Morwena be right? The great I Am sent back to howl with Anubis in the desert? Supplanted by the She! Why not? Wasn't there something in Michelet?

Martha snapped on a light and roamed her shelves until she found *La Sorcière*. She flicked through the pages. All that nonsense about black masses. Ah, here it was, the description of the Woman: 'with a face like Medea, a beauty born of sufferings, a deep, tragic, feverish gaze, with a torrent of black, untamable hair falling as chance takes it, like waves of serpents. Perhaps, on top, a crown of vervain, like ivy from tombs, like violets of death.'

Martha looked in the mirror. Then she began to laugh. She walked to the tall, narrow window, glanced across to the Poltreth headland and the coastguard cottage – the last lights, bright as goodness, before the dark.

She felt the rise within her warmly of a great appetite.

The Allgoods would drive through the night. Gladys went indoors to fetch the thermos. At the last moment, before she climbed into the van, Tess hugged Molly.

'And any of you can come any time. You know that. And we'll be down.'

'I know.'

'Molly, this place – I couldn't. Are you sure?'

For a second Molly thought, I could go, I could simply step into the van and Tess and Humph would take care of me. So long as someone fed him would Walter even notice I had gone?

'I'm fine, love, really.'

'Take care.'

'And you.'

They were all there to wave off the Allgoods. As the tail-lights of the van disappeared, Gladys, Penny and Tinker went indoors. Molly took Walter's arm and he put an arm round her shoulder. Then they went into the warm house, closed the window and pulled the curtains, bolted the door behind them.

SIX

Spring came and went once, twice, three times. A tease of pink on the trees, then just as they had swept out the house, flung open the doors and windows for the paint to dry, the south cone was hoisted, a great gale rushed in. Gladys brought Hazel, her rabbit, indoors. Only the dog Enoch slept outside in his usual spot by the water-butt. The lifeboat maroon, fired twice, startled them awake. Yet by morning the rain and wind had growled off east, leaving the landscape washed, the sky blue as milk.

Gladys had developed an irritating habit of nodding to herself as if someone had said something with which she agreed. She looked in some way smug, thought Molly, but at least she wasn't any more so tiresomely *there*. She went for great tramps along the cliffs or into the woods and came back with cuttings, sometimes roots, of plants she almost certainly should not have picked. Polpody, she said. Spleenwort, Yellow Archangel, Lady Fern.

Tinker said there were magic mushrooms on the moor.

Molly took Jason to the beach and into the woods that embraced the landward end of the harbour. While on the cliffs the rare trees there were had been crippled by the westerlies, here on the forest floor there was a breathing warmth of plants strange and familiar and a thickening scent of wild garlic: foul until you grew accustomed to it.

Molly's dizziness had settled, almost, into an equilibrium. She had now something like a sense of place.

Women, she thought, seemed to need that more than men. When they first came, before she opened her eyes, she was in limbo. Now Wandsworth had faded and she could feel around her the shape of the small bedroom, the wardrobe too big, the

cottage, the harbour below, the cliffs, the path through the trees
to Poltrue. Then she would go to the window. There was the
ferry, the wide ocean, there across the water was Poltrue, the
church spire, the quay, the terrace of Victorian houses with
their witchy pointed roofs, that looked so small from the street
but on the waterside toppled almost down to the sea itself. And
crowning all, the pink-washed blancmange of the Channel Hotel.
Her eye flicked back to the topmost of the terraced houses.

What was real? What was fantasy? Walter had noticed there was
a moment at dusk in certain dying lights when the habitations
and the rocks become one, so this might have been a planet not
unlike our own but hostile, incapable of sustaining life. Or life
had visited it and perished. Or life had not yet arrived. It was
still contemplating that first step from the amniotic waters, to
the beach, to the Garden, to the Fall. If it had known what lay
in store might it have slipped back into the slime? He said
something of the sort to Martha.

'I doubt it,' said Martha. 'Would you have chosen not to be
born?'

Walter pondered. Once he would have been sure of his
answer. Now, standing at the edge of the sea in the cove just
round the headland, Martha's dinghy beached beside *Cleo*, he
had an odd feeling that he would have struggled out of the sea,
lashing his small reptilian tail, if only to be here, with her. He
thought no further than that. He never planned these meetings
but had ceased to be startled by her unlooked-for appearances.
Sailing in, he would know even before he looked up that Martha
was on her terrace and three or four times had skirted the
whirlpool to tie up at the front of the worn granite stairway cut
in the rock. Like a manifestation, she was suddenly there in
the Poltrue Aquarium and they were considering together the
flat-eyed pollack when Gladys and Jason appeared. Walter turned
to introduce them and Martha was gone.

She had been in a gale on the cliffs, walking into the wind,
head uncovered, hair streaming, cloak flying behind her. 'Isn't
it wonderful!' she had shouted and Walter loped beside her for
a mile, purblind with salt spray, before he noticed that old Enoch

had left them. 'Never liked me,' she'd yelled, 'dogs. Or perhaps he can smell my cat.'

She had been in the churchyard on a day of brazen blue, eating sandwiches and sketching in charcoal, bold, slashing strokes that in places tore the paper. While Martha squatted on the edge of a grave her little black cat dozed in the sun beside her. Already, in this sheltered spot, crocus had pricked through the ground, the first blossom was out and egg-faced daffodils. Walter thought it was terrible, how graveyards flourished.

Then she was in the small bay to the west of the harbour-mouth, out to sea. By chance, of course, but Walter realised he would have been disappointed to arrive and not to see Martha's rowing-dinghy pulled up.

'On balance,' he replied, 'I would choose life.' They were standing looking out at the ocean. The entrance to the coomb was narrow – Walter had nearly sailed past it the first time: at their backs was a fall of cliff, no path. Martha stood with her hands in her oilskin pockets. It was a cold, sunny day of danger-ous clarity. Tomorrow there would be rain. He was beginning to learn but knew he would never learn everything there was to know. He had never felt that as sharply as he did here, by the sea. He liked that: the mystery. Last time they were here Martha had shown him a colony of tunicates, those strange jelly-like creatures, more like slugs than fish, with the dorsal nerve cord that linked them to man himself in an evolutionary chain so long it was as hard to comprehend as creation. 'The sea is extraordinary.'

She might have been reading his mind (she had been reading his mind).

'If someone said – here, you can have all the answers, from the beginning to the end, everything, wouldn't you be tempted?'

It sounded like a challenge, the way she put it. She was grinning. Her sharp eye-teeth showed.

'Of course.'

'Why not then? What is the point of ignorance?'

'None, I suppose,' he said. He thought, that was where God might be, in our unknowing. Once he had seen Him as an old man in the sky speaking through the chapel bell, the sounding

organ. Then he was gone. A bell was a bell, the high voices of
the sung Nunc Dimittis a pretty noise like birds swarming against
the vaulted roof. What he felt now was simple-minded, he knew,
but so long as he could hold on to mystery, there God might be
found, in the numinous, in the questions that could not be
answered. Perhaps that was why the sea affected him – it could
never be entirely known. It humbled him.

'I'm sorry – what did you say?'

Martha looked up, shoulder hunched against the wind to light
a cigarette.

'I said the moor used to be under the sea. I've got a cottage
up there. You must come some time. In summer. There are
wonderful pools. Cold. I swim.'

Careful. Watch it. This one's nervy as a virgin.

Martha could imagine Walter's limbs, so white except at the
forearms and the neck. He would have narrow, attenuated feet.
His chest would be hairless. His legs would sport no knotted
veins. Except for that lumbar weakness he was in good shape
for his age. Better than Midwinter, the great I Am. She almost
said: have you ever thought that there is no God, that pure evil
rules in the shape not of the fiend but man? Midwinter grows
feeble as his dominion is usurped.

She said: 'Look, the tide's turned. When I first came here
there were women who believed that the ebb at full moon could
take away all ills. For all I know, they still do.'

Martha flung away her cigarette.

'We'd better get back before it runs too hard. You ought to
look out for an outboard engine. It's a scouring tide.'

'Yes, I will.'

Going back in, Walter sailing on the small puff of wind, Martha
rowing, there was a queer pause in the tide. It might just have
been a contrary current but it was more as if someone had
reached out and held back the ebb.

Gladys had seen them.

Gladys knew more than people gave her credit for.

She didn't say but she could have.

She had been around town. She knew. Here she was not

overlooked. People told her things. Sally in the dairy with a wart on her nose told her the vicar slept with all three daughters, regular. The yacht club vice-commodore wore a bra at Ladies' nights. Pauline in the Lobster Pot café took on the whole lifeboat crew.

Who had cancer though they didn't know it.

Mind you, Pauline's all right. We all need a bit of fun.

What about a spot of clotted?

Which wives swopped husbands. Who killed himself with rum and bleach. Who put her arm down the waste-disposal.

What about a nice cup of tea?

Martha Price? Yes, now you come to mention. All right, for a writer, keeps herself to herself so she gets left alone. No, not much for men, though there was one years ago, didn't stay long. Dapper looking in a dance-hall sort of way, but sickly, I said.

Gladys knew. She'd seen them on the water and the terrace and the beach. Not that Walter ever would. It surprised her he'd managed to marry. We'll bear it in mind, Gladys told Hazel. You never know.

Spring swelled and burst bringing more meetings. (Though not yet Midwinter to England – he had been caught in an hotel fire in Salem, Mass. Once out of intensive care he was the darling of the nurses. Time was, he would have got them all with child. Nice though it was to be spoiled, he mourned the loss of his grosser priapic urges.)

Flowers that in London would have fought for a living here in the west grew wild in crazed abundance and tremendous size. Rhododendrons as tall as trees, great waxy-faced camellias. Bamboo. Plants and shrubs Molly had never seen before. Excess. Even the walls flowered.

Her hands were suddenly empty. Jason crossed by ferry every day to the Poltrue primary school. Penny showed no inclination to go anywhere but lolled around with the twins. She smelled of milk, displayed no curiosity about her surroundings, watched television most of the day and half the night. Enoch, when he wasn't paddling after Walter, stood self-appointed watchdog to the twins when Penny put them out in their double-ended carry-cot. The black dog with the greying muzzle assumed solemn responsibility for these two strange white worms with their waving sea-fingers.

'You know what it means, don't you?' said Tess. The Allgoods came down most weekends to their cottage by the Mission Hall.

Molly shook her head.

'Enoch – God's messenger. Moll, are you sure you're all right?'

'Absolutely fine.'

'But what do you *do*?'

Gladys cooked. Fish pie usually. Fish pie four days a week because Walter said he liked it. Tinker, amazingly, had stayed around, working on the house, and for Molly this was strange. For the first time in her married life, Molly could have sat, if she wished, hands folded while her home took shape around her. White walls, fitted cupboards, kitchen units, sanded floorboards, rush mats. Tinker would disappear for an hour in the van and come back with what looked like rubbish but turned out to be treasure. A fish kettle. A pine table that only needed a scrub. Once a silver soup ladle and a stuffed owl. A lustre jug.

'But wherever do you get them? How do you pay?'

'Dumps. Skips. Nothing.'

'But who would throw them out?'

Tinker talked with his mouth half-full of pasty.

'The dead. This is where people come to drop off their perches, Ma. You must have realised that.'

(Beware! The magpies crowd, at low water there is a stink, graveyards overflow. The West is the place of death. My finger pricks.)

'Of course.' Molly smiled. Went on smiling as she filled the lustre jug, arranged the primroses, thought Walter dead. I would be a madwoman on the edge of a dark cliff.

I could manage the day, I think.

But the night.

Poltreth unnerved Molly sometimes. It was so full of secrets and shadows. At dusk with the clouds flying, she reeled as if the sky were still, the earth alone the single spinning orb. At the only grocer's – everything deep frozen as if it were the shop at the end of the universe – the gossips fell silent when she entered. The silence slapped Molly on the mouth, she lost her voice. Climbing Fore Street it was her breath that went while at her back she heard a door slam like a coffin lid, footsteps, turned, and the road was empty. Corners were sly, walls crazily toppled, windows were mean and watching. There was dizzying beauty at the top, on the cliffs, at her own back door, but below, in the village (which looked so pretty on a postcard), winter was only hiding, not gone – cold fingers reached to pinch from the maze of precipitous alleys and passages cut in the granite, where more than once Molly had lost her way.

'It'll be better at Easter,' Tinker said. He alone seemed to have established a truly social relationship with the place. That is, with the Ferry Inn where the young of Poltreth – not unlike the dog-like youths on the quay at Poltrue – gathered most evenings. Molly walked past the open door one night and saw in the bright indoors Tinker drinking in a huddle with three sharp-shouldered, villainous-looking lads. They spoke, presumably, the common language of youth. One had a shaved head, the other two unfashionably long, black locks. Where did they spring from? What did they do? Not much, Tinker reported, disarming with a grin.

Easter came, biting cold. A flurry of young couples with children and dogs and boxes and boats filled the Mission Hall car-park with Saabs and estate vans and Volvos and Audis. Flung open doors, windows, struggled to light fires. Uncertain, wavering plumes rose from the chimneys of the summer places, then fires were damped down, houses closed again and the heaped cars drove away in a sudden, unseasonal dash of snow that fell on the white faces of the camellias but did not settle.

Poltrue was better. Molly crossed to shop, to meet Jason from school (not that he needed meeting or even liked being met), or to walk in the friendlier woods up to the castle.

'Aren't they lovely! A bit late this year.' Norah Carteret bent over the brimming basket of primroses. 'They do have a scent, don't they. A green smell.'

Molly had met her coming out of the antique shop. They crossed together to the Lobster Pot.

'Did you buy anything?'

'Selling I'm afraid, my dear, not buying.' Norah smiled and stirred her tea. 'The furniture went long ago, of course. This was an opal ring with a diamond setting. Quite pretty.'

'Oh. I'm sorry.'

'No need to be. A compensation of old age is that things don't matter so much any more. I mean possessions. All those years we were in the diplomatic, running around like refugees, I used to think, how wonderful when we have a place of our own. Then in the end, with Gerald as he was, there didn't seem much point. And I didn't mind. We'd dragged those crates all round the world. I just told the sale-room to unpack them and get the best price they could. And d'you know what I felt? Free.' Norah looked at her watch. 'But I'm talking too much.'

'No, please.' (Please, stay, there is a shadow at the corner of my mind.)

'Well, I mustn't be long. I left Gerald in the doctor's waiting-room but I must fetch him. You see, unless people know – about Alzheimer's – they think he's drunk. Most of the time he's a lamb then suddenly he'll start shouting. I do hope.' Norah shook her head.

'Hope what?'

'I just hope he'll go before it gets worse.' Norah looked up and smiled. Molly thought what a pretty woman she must have been. 'I do apologise. I don't usually talk about it. Oh, isn't that Martha Price?'

Molly turned too late.

'Do you know her well?'

'Hardly at all. But an interesting face, don't you think. Not exactly beautiful. Handsome? Some tragedy there, I forget what. She lost a child? A still-birth? No, I think it was an operation. She was gone for a while and looked quite ill when she came back.'

'My husband knows her.'

'*Does* he?' Norah seemed surprised and might have said more but now it was Molly who noticed the time.

'I must go. My grandson –'

She stood, picked up her basket and on an impulse emptied it. 'Please,' she said.

'Oh, my dear!' Molly was gone before Norah could thank her properly. She would have run after her but her lap was full of primroses. Such an abundance. Where would she put them? Would the hotel lend her a vase? She buried her face in their dampness and felt, absurdly, that if she didn't leave at once, she might weep.

'We're doing dinosaurs.'

'Are you, darling?'

Molly had only just caught up with Jason on the ferry. Crossing, they had seen Walter coming in in *Cleo* and waved. They were almost at the top of Fore Street.

'I've got a snake.'

'Where?'

'In this box. I'm going to tell Gladys.'

By the time Molly reached the cottage Jason was on his knees in the yard pulling at the string on a shoebox.

'Jason, what are you talking about? What is that?'

Penny was lolling in the back door. Gladys was beating a rug – one of Tinker's dusty treasures. When Jason called she came over and stood by the box. Molly struggled to catch her breath.

'Gladys, look! I've got a snake!'

There did seem to be something heaving under the damp grass in the shoe-box.

'That's nice.' Gladys watched with interest as a yellowy-green head reared itself. Molly shuddered and stepped back.

'It's not nice at all. Jason, you simply cannot keep a snake.'

'They said I could at school. It's a grass snake. It doesn't bite.'

'Perhaps. But you'll have to feed it. What does it eat?'

'Frogs,' Gladys said. 'Three times a week. Or fish. It'll be hungry. Just out of hibernation.' She turned to Molly. 'That Martha Price telephoned. She invited me to her party.'

'You?'

Jason had the snake out of the box. He was trying to hold it like a baby and stroke it.

Molly said: 'Jason, it's not a cat. They probably don't like being stroked. And what's that awful smell?'

'Well, she said you could take anyone. So I said yes.'

'Jason, it's the snake making the smell. Put it down. You can't possibly keep it anyway.'

'They need water. Can I give it a drink?'

Penny had come to inspect.

'Mmn. Rather pretty. Feels lovely. Stroke it, Ma.'

'Penny, don't encourage him. Jason, put it back in the box and we'll take it down to the copse. There's a stream there. You can go and see it whenever you want to.'

'Can I give it a fish?'

'All right. There's a mackerel in the fridge. Get that and we'll take it to the copse.'

Jason looked up at the adults. For a moment Molly thought there was going to be a tussle, then he shrugged.

'OK. I wanted a dinosaur really, anyway.'

Unusually for her, Molly had a whisky, then another. Walter and Tinker were in the shed working on an adjustment to the boat tiller. Every day Molly expected Tinker to say he was off. He had never stayed so long in one place since he left home. With Hazel at her feet Gladys was knitting. Old Enoch was in the shed with the men. Penny was watching *Psycho II*.

'Penny?'

'Yeah?

'Nothing.'

Penny yawned. It was that bit where you've realised that Norman Bates isn't really cured but the girl hasn't. And she's coming to the house alone. Any idiot could have told her. It wasn't half as good as Hitchcock.

Though she did not identify her mood with the spring, Penny felt restless. There had been a letter from Stan. Well, two £10 notes and a greasy card of Tower Bridge he'd probably nicked. The card was blank, not even an address but she had recognised the backward-sloping writing on the envelope: SWALK. No one did that any more, except Stan. He must be the only man in the world who still did that.

Stan might come. Or she might just take off anyway.

Penny rolled over onto her stomach. They were coming to get Anthony Perkins. Penny wondered vaguely if there was such a thing as evil, if evil was real, like sex.

Tomorrow, Molly thought, I'll get out my painting things. It's not this place, it's not the world, or Walter, or anything but myself.

I simply need something to do.

Tomorrow.

And then there were three days of bland golden weather – more like autumn than spring. Morning mist lifted, the sun seemed painted in the sky, the sea was not only calm but of a blue Molly had never seen north of the Mediterranean.

Walter went out onto the cliff sniffing for wind, as he did every morning. When he found none he took Molly in *Cleo*, motoring with his new outboard round to a bay to the east of the harbour entrance.

Molly sketched or simply sat with her back against a rock.

Walter was so sweet. He might have been apologising for something. He brought her treasure: shells, driftwood, tiny coloured stones like tesserae. She arranged them on the white sand in the shape of a necklace. He cherished her.

'Are you warm enough?'

'Oh yes,' Molly closed her eyes. Perhaps that was all she had needed: the sun on her face. The open sea. 'Walter?'

He was standing at the sea's edge, a jagged scrawl of a figure against the ocean and the sky. Oh, she did love him. Marriage, she thought: a beautiful word. Like carriage, faintly scented with philadelphus. She slept, woke feeling happier than she had since they came here.

They went back in at the time of day when, in still weather, the reflection of the shadowed rocks and houses of Poltreth became great castles and battlements under water, pictures under glass. Then the ferry scuttled past and the picture was smashed.

'The first of May,' someone was saying. 'Beltane. They used to burn the witches.'

'Also the time when witches were at their most powerful,'
Morwena answered. Martha hadn't asked her but she had come
all the same. She was making quite a hit with the local amateur
archivist – an etiolated fellow with a blob of cotton wool on his
chin. Martha had met him at the Regional Studies Centre in the
course of pursuing Fenny Trevanion. Morwena, in red and
bangles, was positively flirting with him. It had been the same
when they were children. Anything Morwena saw she wanted
then when she'd got it was bored at once and broke it. Well,
the wretched man would have to look after himself.

'Midwinter was so sorry,' Morwena had hissed. 'He has such
happy memories of this dump.'

'Don't remind me.' Martha had propped the door open but
the first-comers knocked or rang all the same. She left Morwena
enchanting the wretched Godfrey and went to refill the dip.
Cucumber, paprika and something a little special. When she
went to buy the yoghurt Sally from the dairy had offered to help
(interesting – I'd been right about the wart) and brought along
her sister, Selina. Sally carried around the celery and dip. Selina
helped to mix the punch and now to serve it.

Half an hour before the party started Martha was wishing
profoundly she had never thought of it. While the girls worked
in the basement kitchen ('You go and make yourself pretty, my
dear', Sally had said), she had gone to the sleeping gallery,
gulped half a tumbler of vodka and surveyed her wardrobe. The
Syrian silk was crumpled in the corner and greasy round the
neck. All that remained besides everyday trousers, long brown
skirts and fish-smelling smocks, was a Hashemite kaftan. The
black did nothing for her complexion and the garment felt much
too heavy but in the end she pulled it on, fumbled with the
frog-fastenings in gold thread, caught her hair in an elastic band,
slashed on her only lipstick (purple) without looking in the mirror
(what was the point when she had no reflection?), and snatched
up the heavy silver serpent bracelet, trying to forget who had
given it to her (Midwinter).

The first half hour had been sticky but now the punch was
doing its job and by the time the Watermans arrived the party
had very nearly reached shouting point. Few of the guests could

be said to know their hostess but most knew each other. Molly knew no one and was thankful to see that Norah Carteret had come after all. There were, of course, Walter, who had astonished Molly by changing into his one good cord suit without any fuss; and Gladys – quite amazingly sporting a beehive ginger hair-do and pink velour track suit. She plunged into the party as if she'd been doing it all her life. Again to Molly's surprise Penny had announced at the last moment that she might go after all. She left the children with Tinker and came downstairs looking like Cinderella after the ball.

'I thought you were changing,' Molly said.

'I have.'

There she was now, lounging against the wall eating cocktail sausages and chewing the sticks. She was wearing what appeared to be rags, vaguely the colour of seaweed. No make-up, of course, though she had heaped her pale hair on top of her head and stuck in it a few spring flowers, already wilting. A sketch for that girl in the Botticelli *Primavera*, thought Molly. (Just occasionally, Molly had had an urge to shake her daughter. But it would have made no difference. Penny would simply have shrugged and gone back to watching television.)

'Have you seen your father?'

'He's over there with that peculiar woman in the black sack.'

'I think that's our hostess.' Molly sipped thankfully at her punch. 'Aren't you enjoying yourself?'

'It's all right. But they're all so old, aren't they. Dinosaurs.' Penny took a stick of celery and left Molly with a parting shot. 'I think you ought to keep an eye on Pops.'

'I'm enjoying myself so much, aren't you? How nice to see you, my dear.'

Norah Carteret was looking very pretty in blue if a little flushed from the heat or the punch. Or perhaps from her daring at leaving Gerald. He had been rather a lamb today, in fact, almost as if he understood and didn't mind. Norah had read him one of Susan's short and rare letters as she always did but this time, after a pause and much struggle, he had managed to say 'Susan'. 'That's right, darling,' Norah had said, taking his hand,

'Susan's in New Zealand.' 'New Zealand,' he said. That's what Alzheimer's did, turned you into a parrot.

'One of the chamber-maids promised she'd look in so Gerald should be all right. This room is rather extraordinary, isn't it? They must have taken out a floor. And there's a spiral staircase up to that gallery, and down to the basement. Have you seen that woman in red with an American accent? I wonder who she is. Am I talking too much?'

Molly smiled and shook her head. 'Not at all.'

'I'm not used to people, you see, so it's rather fun. Well, there is the club but that's not really people. Don't you think parties are interesting? Everyone talking but no one saying anything. But then no one ever does, I suppose. Say what's in their heads. That's all secret – what really matters.'

Molly nodded. Over Norah's shoulder she was looking for Walter.

'Excuse me.'

The shy spring evening light had faded. The windows were black now, mirrors reflecting the dimly candled room. Molly took another glass of punch and set off in the direction she had last seen Walter. At the furthest corner she paused.

(Those windows are too high. Where does the ceiling go?) She was trying to make out the Poltreth headland and the bright windows of the coastguard cottage but one of those sudden westerly winds had whipped in, bringing rain, and the world outside this room shivered on the edge of dissolving: land, lights, home.

Something against her ankle. Alive. Like fur.

'I'm sorry, did he make you jump? That's my cat. I'm Martha Price.'

'I'm Molly Waterman.'

'I know. I'm glad you came. To tell you the truth, I wasn't sure anyone would come at all.'

At first sight all Molly had taken in was the woman's tall, blackly triangular shape. A long, sallow face. Then Martha smiled and Molly found herself thinking: there is something wonderful about this woman.

'Come here, you beast.' Martha scooped up the small black

cat. It swore and jumped from her grasp. 'Not used to parties. Neither am I.'

Were her eyes a very dark brown or black? And that dress – or kaftan rather – accounted for the triangular lines. A hard, thick, slubbed cotton with the sheen of silk. Molly felt dowdy in her flower-patterned skirt with the cheap black top from Elsie's in Fore Street. And the woman seemed to have a smell – not exactly a scent but something oily, faintly musky.

Martha was watching her. Some response seemed to be expected. Not so much watching perhaps, as studying. The windows rattled. The gale was getting up. Molly shivered.

'This is a beautiful house.'

'Would you like to see it?'

'Thank you.' As she followed Martha down the spiral staircase, Molly glanced back. There was Walter on the far side of the room a head above the rest. Was that Gladys who had him pinned against the wall? That bouffant hair-do bouncing up and down?

Martha was saying: 'No upstairs, you see, just the gallery. This is a sort of kitchen-cum-everything. Oh, there you are, Pounce. Phew. Do sit down. Shove those papers out of the way. I had to clear my desk for drinks.'

She was pushing around the mess on the big table and finally came up with a battered packet of cigarettes. She lit one and only then pushed the pack in Molly's direction. Molly noticed that her rather beautiful long fingers were nicotine-stained. The nails were jagged in places and unvarnished. Her hands looked strong, more like a man's. Molly shook her head and Martha gave her that crooked grin again.

'I'm the only one left.' She surveyed the room. 'What a muck. Sorry.'

I think she's nervous too, thought Molly.

'I like it. The room, I mean.' Haircord on the floor the colour of earth, black range on which there bubbled a heavy, cast-iron pot, a fish-smoker, bundles of dried herbs, demi-johns against the wall, some empty, some full, clutter left over from the preparations for a party. In front of the range the small black cat with the red collar, neat and straight as a pot cat, half-dozing, half watching Molly.

'I'm sure I've seen your cat before.'

'Oh, Pounce. He gets everywhere.' Abruptly, Martha stood. 'Let's have a proper drink.'

The liquid from the stone jar was yellow, nearly colourless. It tickled Molly's nasal passages and for a second she found it unpleasant. The aftertaste might have been honey or mead.

'My own scrumpy,' Martha said. 'Foul. But quite a kick.'

'It has.' Molly, dizzy, then warm, had difficulty for a moment in focusing. She closed her eyes and opened them, found a place for her glass among the papers. There was something she had meant to say. About Walter? Whatever it was had slipped her mind. 'Walter said you were researching a book.' Come to think of it, that was all Walter had said about Martha Price.

'Yes.' Martha refilled Molly's glass. 'Have you heard of Fenny Trevanion?'

'No.'

'A witch. Hanged at Launceston in 1648. Not burned. That was only in Scotland.'

'How awful. What was she accused of?'

Martha reached for the cigarette packet, found it empty, crumpled it and ranged in strides about her kitchen, opening cupboards, drawers, finally pouncing on a pack almost as battered from which she took what appeared to be the last cigarette.

'Everything in the book. Aborting the unborn of Bodmin by miscarriage. Killing cattle. Wrecking. Keeping a familiar. Wenching unnaturally in the guise of a vixen. What I'm trying to find out is how much was true. A good deal, I think.'

'True? Surely –'

'It's a common fallacy that all the witches were innocent old biddies.' That wonky smile again. 'There's a witch in every woman. No man could understand how close women are to the earth, the tides, the moon, to nature. Women *are* nature.'

(A bird flings itself against the window. A plate breaks. Seas of blood. Seas and seas of blood.)

'I think I see what you mean.' (Molly doesn't want to look.) 'Up to a point.'

'Sorry. It's my hobby-horse. If not one of my choosing. Rather boring.' The kitchen tipped and returned to the horizontal. It was just as though the plates on the shelves of the oak dresser had rushed to one end then righted themselves. For that same period of time (how long? the blink of an eyelid? an hour?) Molly had the illusion of spying on Martha, of seeing the whole room through the wrong end of a telescope.

Martha was saying: 'Witches are greatly misunderstood. Wax dolls, pins, potions, all those toys are sorcerer's stuff.' The cat had jumped onto Molly's lap, regarded her with its yellow eyes, turned round three times pawing for the best position, and settled. 'Pounce's taken to you. That's unusual. Tell me, how do you find people here?'

'I don't know so many.'

'Nor do I and I've lived here years. You won't get far at Poltreth. They're very close there.' Molly sneezed. 'Are you allergic to cats? Chuck him off.'

'No. No, I don't think so. I never have been. I've been wanting to ask you about your novel. I can't find it in the library.'

This time Martha threw back her head and laughed. Pounce stopped purring and looked up sharply. It was more like a bark than a laugh.

'You won't. It was rather naughty. Set here – or that's what the dodos thought. The real locals couldn't care less. I was sent to Coventry so I went to Egypt. I believe the club are still huffy about it but since I never go there that doesn't matter. Anyhow, better get back to my party, I suppose. If it's still there. Down, Pounce.'

The little cat arched its back, stretching, and followed its mistress. At the bottom of the spiral staircase Martha turned.

'You paint, don't you?'

'Well, I did.'

'Did your husband tell you I was thinking of starting a group? For the women, if I can get enough. I do hope you'll come.'

Martha's gaze was extraordinarily peremptory.

'Thank you. Perhaps I could think about it.'

'Of course.'

The party had peaked and begun to thin out. Those left were

talking in small clusters, some sitting. Gladys's unused laugh
startled Molly. She was talking to that woman in red with the
bangles. The man with cotton wool on his chin was hovering.
He wore the foolish expression of a hopeful dog waiting to be
walked. A second man had joined them. A dapper fellow, unlike
the rest of the men dressed formally, in an expensive-looking
dark suit. Black hair with a flash of silver at the sides. White
cuffs. A stain on his cheek – birthmark? Burn?

The American-sounding woman called out.

'Martha, look who's here! He made it after all.'

'Damn.' From behind her Molly heard Martha draw in her
breath.

'Ma?'

'Penny.' The wobble had set in again. There seemed to be a
tilt to the floor. Molly felt as if she were climbing a hill.

'Ma I think you're pickled.'

'Just a bit hot. Where's your father?'

'Where did you go? You were hours.'

'To look downstairs. Oh. Walter. I think we should go. You'd
better get Gladys. Is it raining?'

They had all brought oilskins.

'Sorry about the weather,' Martha called after them. She
stood in the light of the door, her cat on her shoulder as
they plunged, wind and weather at their backs, down to the
ferry.

The small boat bucked and had to make three passes before
it could land them.

Tinker was sitting with his feet up in front of the fire.

'Well, Glad? Coach turned back into a pumpkin?'

'I could go to America,' Gladys said. The crossing had tipped
her beehive and half undone it. She went to her bedroom and
looked in the mirror. It was disappointing not to see reflected
there the new Gladys who had been to a party and talked to a
lot of people. All the same there was plenty to think about.
Regretfully she took off the track suit, put on her nightie, washed
her face with soap and water and brushed her hair fifty times.
Well, perhaps she wasn't a beehive person really. She said her
prayers and climbed into bed. She slept at once and her dreams

were remarkable. If the waking Gladys could be the Gladys of her dreams she'd make them all sit up.

Norah had been absurdly relieved to find Gerald just as she left him, wearing pyjamas and dressing-gown, watching the television. It was only when she was crossing the road and climbing the short hill to the Channel Hotel that she had been seized by panic; by the fear, the near-certainty, that something terrible had happened. She walked so fast up and against the wind that she tripped on the kerb and fell, quite painfully, on her knee. The street was empty. With no one to help her she could be here all night. It was only with the greatest effort that she managed at last to stand, to pick up her umbrella (pointless to open it in this wind) and use it as a walking stick to cover the last hundred yards to the hotel. It was hard to breathe. As the trees creaked wickedly and a branch snapped with the sound of a bone cracking, the thought came to Norah, for the first time admitted, that she might go first – and then what would become of Gerald?

Then, after the panic (what a wild crow they must have thought downstairs, silly old woman hardly making sense, something the storm blew in), Gerald had not fallen off his chair, smashed the windows, set fire to himself, gone off into everlasting night.

In the tiny bathroom Norah drank water from a tooth-glass (sip, don't gulp) and sank onto the closed lavatory lid. Her breathing was steadier now and she had stopped shaking enough to pull off the stocking – torn and bloody at the knee. No grit under the skin, thank heaven. Quite a swelling but that will go down. Reach for the flannel, soap and water, wash it clean. Now, don't make a fuss, Norah, only boobies cry when they fall down. If you stand, holding onto the side of the bath and then the cupboard, you can reach the iodine. That did hurt. Sit back a bit while the sting goes off, close your eyes. Remorse is the enemy of content. Now where did I see that? True, anyway, like most platitudes. Sampler virtues perpetuated in cross-stitch. Yet she did feel guilty. Before one could get rid of a feeling one had to recognise it. All the same, in acknowledging that wave

of fear before she fell (the fear that felled her?) she found no
relief, only a return of the terror. Her hands shook so much she
dropped the iodine in reaching into the cupboard for a box of
plasters. Now she would have to tip the chambermaid. That
was, if anything could be done to get out the stain. There had
been a little trouble with the manager already about that shade
Gerald broke when he knocked over the lamp. He indicated then
that they were allowed to stay strictly on sufferance. If Gerald's
condition were to worsen. If he were to behave in any way that
disturbed the guests. If Norah could no longer cope. As it was,
the district nurse had to come in through the servants' entrance.

At last in bed, Norah sorted through her library books but
even P. D. James could not hold her (so reliable as a rule in
removing one from tedious circumstances). She picked up
Susan's letter as though simply to touch it might summon her
daughter from the other side of the world. No longer her
daughter: a sensible woman and bad letter-writer who would be
embarrassed were Norah to reply in the terms that came first
to mind (I love you, I know you cannot return this love but there
was a time when you did and that was the best of my life). Which
took Norah back to the conversation with Molly Waterman at
the party. That sense of the interior lives people have. The only
true life, and all that effort to cover it up. Such a waste of spirit.

Just for once, perhaps, one of Gerald's sleeping pills. Think
of something nice. The party. The blue had looked quite good
and she was glad that Sandra had persuaded her to have a lighter
perm. That was the look nowadays – natural. Molly Waterman's
husband seemed very nice. Rather shy. Norah had the
impression that, like her, he was not a party-goer. For a moment
she hadn't recognised the Gladys person. Then there had been
the woman from America and the rather distinguished man who
arrived towards the end. Martha Price had not looked too
pleased to see him. Now there was an interesting face – Martha
Price's. Very striking but tragic. She had said something about
a group she was starting, if Norah might be interested.

Gerald called out in his sleep, thrashed as though to break
out of some painful constraint. With difficulty, dizzy from the pill
and the fall, Norah lowered herself from her bed and, keeping her

balance with one hand on the table between them, straightened Gerald's bedclothes. He mumbled and opened his eyes but still in dream. 'Hush,' Norah said.

Poor Gerald. Back in her bed, there was a thought formulating in Norah's mind. About Gerald. Illness. The illness a stronger bond even than marriage. Then images. The blue of her frock, her mother dressed for a garden party, brothers, cousins, Susan; the living and the dead all gathered together in a field, in one harvest of souls. The last vision Norah had that night was of Martha Price's face.

'She's beautiful, isn't she?' Molly said.

Walter turned his head on the pillow.

Molly was looking at the ceiling. 'I mean she has marvellous features. I wonder if she's sexy.' No use asking Walter. Might as well talk to a blind man.

'Mmn.'

'I think she's probably lonely, don't you? Well, you know her better. We had a rather extraordinary conversation. She's a bit alarming too, isn't she?'

Walter had gone to sleep.

'I thought Morwena said you were in traction or something.' All but one of the candles had burned down. A mercy, thought Martha, rocking and smoking, Pounce in her lap. Midwinter sat in the high black chair by the empty hearth. All she could see was the white flash of his cuffs with their jewelled studs. For once in her life she wished her sister had stayed.

'Burns, my dear, not bones. Stark naked every bit of me for a week in a sort of fish-tank. The water treatment.'

'Your own fire?'

'Certainly not. Arson has never been one of my games.'

His bark in the desert was terrible but in his present manifestation the wretched man did have a rather beautiful voice. That must have been one reason she had ever been attracted to him, Martha thought. Never again. She sighed, loosened her hair and rocked back. The movement eased the tension in her back and neck. To see Midwinter sitting at her hearth as though by right

brought back memories she could hardly bear. A little passion
– oh yes, moments – but at what a price! Her wombless body
remembered the horror and the pain. The loss too: that was a
grief like rain through all her days. (But to have carried it to full
term, brought it to birth . . .)

Abruptly Martha sat up straight, startling Pounce. Her heavy
kaftan creaked.

'What do you want? Why are you here?'

'Surely Morwena told you? I am to address your Ladies'
Dinner Club.'

'Not my ladies. When? I thought you were doing a tour.'

'Alas, it will be a while before I can get about.' He touched
his cheek. 'My face needs to heal. So, the summer here, I
thought, my talk in the fall, then a signing tour. We'll be into a
second edition by then. The University of Sussex have particularly asked me to speak.'

'There's nothing for you here.'

'But I have the fondest memories of Poltrue –'

'In this house. In England. Nothing.'

'I'm only too aware, my dear, that my prime function has been
superseded.'

'We are in hell without your help.'

'All I ask is a pause before I go forth. Is that too much?'

Martha bit her fingernails. That bloody cat had left her. Was
circling his ankles. Silk socks. He always wore silk socks.

'Do what you like. Get out of this house.'

'Where do I go? At this time of night?'

'The Channel Hotel. There's a night porter.'

'Our pact?'

'We never had one.'

'As you wish.'

Martha opened the door. Midwinter went out. The gale blew
in. Pounce mewed after him.

'Damn toady cat.'

The wind blew all night. Martha could see the windows blow
in before it. Glass. Extraordinary. Liquid and sharp at the same
time. Cutting and yielding.

Selina had said she would come in the morning but to get

Midwinter from her mind Martha emptied ashtrays, washed glasses. She broke one, cut herself, sucked her finger, wished she could weep. The lights of Poltreth had gone out. Was it Walter she wanted or his innocence? And Molly? She had felt a sistership with her yet if Molly were her rival then she must surely be her victim? Questions for another day.

Fifty times Martha brushed her hair before the mirror and fifty times the glass gave back no reflection.

> *Or was that a shape, dimly forming?*
> *What happens if it does, if I can see myself?*
> *Shall I be beautiful?*
> *Will the glass*
> *crack?*

SOLSTICE

SEVEN

With the spring Bank Holiday in early May came a punishment of hail from a blue sky, so that the trippers walked bent at the back like penitents in their showerproof cloaks over summer shorts and dresses, trailing their children behind them. The narrow streets of Poltrue were clogged by these dream-walkers who toiled even up Poltreth's hill. At the top most surveyed the endless cliffs and turned back. A few paused, exhausted or dazed by beauty. The light was air, the air light, the sea-light made a fantasy of headlands, put reality in doubt, so that this high promontory with its under-sea granite fingers, might have been a place for a last stand, the end of everything.

'What's that?' Molly said, one hand on Walter's arm, the other pointing. 'It looks like a whale. That rock? Or is it an island?'

'A rocky island. Gwancarrek. When the tide's right you can land there.'

'Have you?'

He shook his head. Molly thought, he has this other life, this sea-life, whatever. We both look at the same view. What we see is not the same.

Walter patted her hand (like patting a dog, Molly said to herself).

He offered: 'We could take a picnic there.'

'We?'

'As many as we can get into *Cleo.*'

'We'll see.'

Molly and Jason had been taken out once for a sail. Except for the earlier outing in the false spring, Molly had never been on the sea before in anything smaller than a Channel ferry. Once they left the harbour a breeze had come up and the sky clouded over. What had struck her was the irrationality of the ocean, the lack of point or purpose behind its temper. The tide rising or falling she could understand. But that bucketing wave that came up over the bows to slap you in the face with cold water. The heave of the swell. A wall of rain had momentarily blotted out all sign of land. Then Jason was sick – surprising himself, it seemed, though he had been ashen since they left the harbour – and Walter put the boat about. Capriciously then the movement was immediately kindly, the tide shouldering them gently home. Walter eased the sheet, the sail filled and Jason regained his colour.

'Does Pops really know what he's doing?' Penny asked. Gladys had cast on for her and with thick, wooden needles Penny had begun to knit some unidentifiable garment in wool like rope.

'In the boat? More or less, I suppose. But I wish he wouldn't go out so far.'

Penny frowned at her knitting.

'I don't know how you stand it.'

'What?'

'Him. Father. Our father. I mean, he's never here. And when he is he's not here really. He never has been.'

'Nor is Stan.'

'That's different.'

'Yes, Stan is different.' Molly smiled. Stan, Stan, Caliban. The phantom plumber and progenitor. She felt more cheerful.

Penny wouldn't let the subject drop. She turned her knitting round, stuck out her tongue and started a new row.

'Damn. I hate purl. What I mean is, I love Pops but doesn't it get you down?'

'Walter? Sometimes. Not so much now.' In saying this, she realised it to be true. 'There are all kinds of love, after all. People change.'

'He'll never change.'

'No, probably not.'

Change? thought Molly. She sorted her painting equipment, put it in the big canvas beach-bag with the money for the ferry. The Allgoods had not been down lately and every week Tess had rung to tell Molly she could not possibly stay in that terrible place. Last night Molly had hung up on her.

Now she set out for the ferry. Well, of course, people didn't change really, not at a deep level. But there were choices and they could be made. And there was nature's example. After the hail and the trippers and Jason's half-term, the weather had produced a miracle. The sun shone, touched faces, flowers, smiles. Even the cliff bloomed. What had been a threatening abundance so unnaturally early had settled into a wonderful flowering. Buddleia in the gardens of Poltreth where nothing but cabbage stalks had drooped. A haze of butterflies. Cowslip in the woods, violets everywhere, the scent of may (unlucky: bring not indoors).

Molly hummed as she made her way down Fore Street. Mutabilitie all about I see.

Walter woke sweating. He dreamed of Martha. Martha haunted him.

Martha had not come to the beach for a week. The strange thing was that her absence was more powerful even than her presence. He would hear her voice and turn, but it was only the wind. He would see the corner of her cloak, once in a puddle her face with that sharp-toothed smile.

Now and then he imagined that Gladys was watching him.

Then his back went and for several days now he had had to rest it. No sailing. He slept again on his mat on the bedroom floor. He watched Molly walking down to the ferry with her canvas beach-bag.

Jason was at school. His red plastic dinosaur lay in the short grass behind the yard. Wincing, Walter stooped to pick it up, one hand in the small of his back.

On the other side of the house, away from the sea, Tinker was digging what might become a vegetable plot. A few yards from Walter Gladys was hanging washing on the line, counting her friends as she pegged out the clothes. One (Walter's longjohns) for Sally, one (Jason's pyjama bottoms) for Selina, one (her own nightie, flowered, frilly and quite low cut) for Sandra. She sang as she pegged: Sally, Selina, Sandra, one, two, three.

Walter found Jason's dinosaur pop-up book and an empty exercise book. He settled in the sun. He had cut himself shaving.

He might grow a beard.

Sometimes he wrote. Jottings.

I am an unfinished man.

Sometimes he read.

The mesosaur was an aquatic dinosaur that laid its eggs in protective shells and so was equipped for living on the land. Yet it never left the water.

Walter tried to think what his stern Darwinist father would have said. Evolution getting ready?

No God, father had announced, banging the Sunday dining-table. No God, boy! (The astonished joint leaked blood.) The universe is nothing but an accident! There was Walter's father in his Sunday suit for not going to church standing at the cliff edge. What are you made of, boy? he shouted and answered himself: the carbon of dead stars. (For the bank he had a second-best suit and for fossil-hunting thick cords that squeaked and smelled of earth. Long walks on cold Dorset shores. Walter got his stoop, perhaps, following father, patrolling Chesil Beach in search of ammonites. Only lately, only since they came here, had he begun to look up.)

Enoch settled at Walter's feet, nose on paws, and Walter scratched the old dog's head.

Father at his shoulder now, dying. Bury me, boy. The last rasp: bury me without box, feed damned worms. Uncoffined he had gone into the earth.

The most terrible dreams of feasting worms.

Gladys was talking to Jason's snake. It had returned from the copse, tempted by Gladys. The Columbrinae, or grass snakes, insist upon live prey but Gladys persuaded it to come to the yard for Whiskas, eggs and milk. It seemed to Walter to have grown. It must be three feet long now, perhaps more. The great worm.

Walter closed his eyes. Walter, are you awake? they always used to say and he would keep his eyes shut. Homo habilis equipped in every way to live, so filled with yearning yet so fearful of that first step.

Walter had slumped in the chair. His hand that had held Jason's book touched the grass. Enoch nosed it gently and Walter smiled. To put aside remorse for uncommitted sins, to cease to watch for the sign that would never come out of the bland sky; to forget questions. Just once to dare. To be!

He thought it was Martha's laugh but it must have been a gull.

'Not bad.' Martha put her head on one side to survey Molly's sketch of the Poltreth headland. There was the cliff, the Watermans' cottage, the swing. And were those tiny creatures Walter and Gladys? Awful. Molly pulled a face. Smiled.

Martha, Molly and Norah were sitting in the sun on Martha's terrace. After a week's silence following the party Martha had telephoned them both to say that maybe they would like to come Tuesday morning? Something had come up (damned Midwinter!) and she wasn't sure about the group but perhaps they could talk about it. And if they had any work they would like to bring?

Norah had nearly refused. Then an old crony of Gerald's had offered to sit with him and the doctor said her leg could do with a little exercise. Nothing too strenuous. And how was Norah in herself, apart from the leg? She must live her own life a bit, get out on her own. Well, she left the number and it was only a hundred yards or so down the hill. It was amazing how the good weather had almost banished the horror of that night of storm. And now it really was rather fun. Once you get over her strangeness, Martha was in her own way immensely hospitable. At midday white wine and now a quite delicious picnic luncheon. Pâté. Goat cheese. Those nice Marks & Spencer biscuits, and fruit.

Martha, in jeans and smock, her hair tied back, refilled their glasses and sprawled in the deckchair, bare feet propped on the wall. There was a wild untrained vine, an early-budding clematis.

Norah was surprised to hear herself say: 'When you come down to it, women are really much more interesting than men.'

Martha flung an apple core over the wall. An attendant gull observed, scorned fruit, screeched and regarding them sideways from that enormous green eye, continued to hover.

'Well, of course they are.' Morwena flicked into Martha's mind. At the party her sister had hissed that the girls were definitely sueing Midwinter for all that Devil-pact rubbish in his new bestseller. It seemed to Martha that there were few creatures more absurd than menopausal Connecticut witches. 'What I don't understand is the militants. We always had the power anyway. That's why the men killed us when they could. They're still afraid. Mind you –' a wide grin '– they have their uses.' She lit a cigarette and blew out the smoke in a plume.

'No stamina though. Have you noticed? They usually die first. And if they don't they can't cope without a woman.'

Molly remembered that strange conversation at the party. What a long time ago that seemed. Yet nothing had changed but her mood.

'I suppose we are closer to nature if only because we give birth.' Too late she recalled, Norah had told her something about Martha. A lost baby? Martha however seemed unworried. She nodded.

'Not just that. Most women have powers they don't recognise or never use. Urges men know nothing about and if they did, wouldn't understand. They sense them though.' Watch it, she told herself. They're not ready, not nearly ready yet. May never be.

Norah blushed like a girl.

'You're right. Do you know, there are times when I feel quite *wicked*.' She regarded the other two anxiously but neither seemed shocked. 'I mean wicked for wickedness's sake. Isn't that frightful? I've never said that before.' Delivered of her confession she felt both alarmed and excited.

'Hecate is in every one of us,' Martha said.

'Oh, do you think so? Yes, I suppose that's right. I never thought of it like that.' The church clock chimed and Norah glanced at her watch. 'Is that really the time? It has gone fast. I've enjoyed myself so much.' So she had.

'And we haven't said a word about your group, my dear. Not that I can imagine anything I could contribute. Perhaps you could teach us something? Your writing?'

I could teach you something indeed, thought Martha, but I shan't.

'Let's not bother about that. Just get together when we feel like it. Call it a sisterhood if you like.'

'Oh, I do like that.'

'Well then.'

Martha stood to show her out. As she picked up her handbag and pulled her cardigan round her shoulders Norah remembered.

'Do tell me. I meant to ask you. That rather handsome man at your party – I could have sworn I saw him in the hotel. But I expect I'm wrong.'

Martha hesitated for only a second, just long enough for a small bruise-coloured cloud to appear in the west.

'No, that's Midwinter.'

'Not the writer? Wasn't he going to talk to the dinner club about the occult?'

'He does write. Among other things.'

'His face seemed familiar.'

'Yes. He's been to Poltrue before. Years ago.'

They had walked through the cavernous room, out of the bright sun, to the small front door.

'So he's in the Channel Hotel now?'

'For the moment. In the Ocean Suite. Well, that tower above the Ocean Suite.'

'The Principessa –'

'An old friend.' Was Martha's parting smile slightly wolfish? If so, Norah did not notice. Leaning not too heavily on her stick, she made her way up the hill. It was her pride to go straight up. Not for her the crabwise route of the elderly. If that was Daphne Mount coming down with her dreadful dog she would cut her. Dead.

Molly had screwed up her first attempt at the view of Poltreth and pushed it in her bag. Her second try was promising to be equally disappointing.

'Ever tried charcoal?'

Martha reappearing on the terrace made Molly jump before she could cover the sketch.

'It's been too long. And I was never much good.'

'Here. Charcoal. Don't worry, I make it myself. Look.'

Martha's spare, imperative line summoned the black face of the cliff, the claw of rock so famous for drownings. Two lines for the cottage crouching near-flat against the west, one for the telegraph pole.

'You really want a bigger pad.'

'But that's marvellous.'

Martha's hand on the pad. In the afternoon heat the smoky, musky scent of her as she crouched by Molly's deckchair. Just for that moment an intense, asexual closeness. Then Martha stood. With the sun behind her, she looked like a tall boy not yet settled into his stretched bones.

'It's not. That's as far as I can go, you see. But it might be somewhere for you to start.'

'Yes. I think I can see that. It might be. Thank you.'

Martha shrugged and flopped back into her lounger. Molly put her pad aside. Both women raised their faces to the sun, closed their eyes against it. I am happy, Molly thought. As if I had held my breath since we came here and now can let it out. I had no idea before how lonely I was.

'It is lovely here.'

'The Land of Nod. Yes.'

'I'm not sure about Walter. Perhaps he expected too much.'

'Have you seen the moor?'

'No.'

'Come to my cottage. Would you like that?'

'Yes. Thank you.'

'You'll come then? Bring the others. Anyone.'

Later Martha's little black cat appeared, complained, and settled on the terrace wall. Martha brought out lemon tea, plucked and bruised a sprig of mint for each tall glass. Molly nearly said: I was frightened of you at first.

'How's Fenny Trevanion?'

The ash grew on Martha's cigarette, a grey worm.

'Rather weird actually. I mean, I haven't done much lately but there's one lead I've got to get back to. Apparently at the last moment on the gallows she repented. That wouldn't mean much on its own but the puzzle is that by then she had nothing to gain.

It's a dubious source and it could be wrong. I may give up the whole thing.'

'I hope not. Well. I must go.'

The sun had all but left the terrace. The cat had moved along the wall and appeared to doze in the last golden puddle. All the light was in the water now and just beginning to touch the windows of west-facing Poltreth. Aegina and Sunion. The dark sister and the fair.

When Molly had gone Martha dragged her deckchair into the corner of sunlight by the terrace wall. She had brought out the Fenny Trevanion papers in the coffee-stained file and took out a photocopied page.

I, Richard Rashlay, do give my testament as Clerk to the Witchfinder that Fenny Trevanion was this day hanged. I say now that I would they had not done this nor I stood witness though I do believe her guilty, both by evidences and the Devil's teat on her nose. By this time after her testings and trial she was blind and near-deaf and plagued with boils which with her age would surely soon have taken her off without benefit of rope. Repentance would not win her life for she knew herself convict and all the peoples were zealously calling for the hangman's work, in the while pelting her and shouting most loudly against her. Yet at the last she did so piteously cry her contrition, for a wonder all the folk were quiet. Then she was dropped and there was a great sigh. It is said that as the breath left her, her spirit put on the shape of a black Cat that ran from the gallows and is even now hunted by the town's people for its torment and death. I pray only that the Lord heard her and took her Soul to Him . . .

Martha sat for a while unmoving, then shivered. At this time of year the shade, after sun, was cold. Yet surely not so cold? She looked across the water where the sun had gone, to Poltreth. Then up on the Poltrue side to the point where she could just glimpse the turret that fancifully crowned the Channel Hotel.

Damn telephone.

'Morwena?'

'Did I disturb you, darling?'

'What do you want?'

'Just to thank you for a lovely party. We did enjoy it. Sorry we had to leave.'

'We?' Martha rubbed her eyes, sighed and sank onto the floor by the telephone.

'Godfrey and I. You can't have forgotten him. Your archivist.'

'Not mine. Morwena, what have you done with him?'

'Nothing you wouldn't enjoy.'

'You simply cannot take people like that.' Martha groaned.

'We're just popping over to the Coast. I hope you're not becoming a prig, Martha. I always felt you had the makings of a prude. And how's dear Midwinter? Can I have a word with him?'

'Go to hell, Morwena.'

Walter was asleep, Enoch at his feet. A book had slipped from his hand. Molly bent to kiss him, wondered whether to wake him to watch the sunset. Then it was too late. It was gone. Molly sneezed.

As the sea swallowed the sun Midwinter finished shaving round the pinkish burn-patch. He had been unaccountably tired lately. He had the impression his blood ran thinner. Did his breath smell? He breathed into his palm and sniffed. Appearances were important. England had never really suited him. Too temperate.

Norah had settled Gerald with a nice prawn and Hellman's sandwich and *EastEnders*. Just time to get to the library. Tuesday was their late night. She cut Daphne Mount again, going up this time, with poor Duggy like a dog on a lead.

Here it was. 'Hecate (hek-u-tee): daughter of the Titans Perses and Asteria. A powerful goddess for good or evil in heaven and on earth. Later associated with Persephone as goddess of the underworld and of magic. Also with Artemis as goddess of moonless nights and crossways.'

Reference. Not to be taken out. No matter. Absently Norah

changed her library books. It had been an interesting day. She had a sense of her life opening. Liver-Wednesday tomorrow. Never mind.

Late into the night, in the Ocean Suite of the Channel Hotel, Midwinter played with the Principessa. Stud poker was their game. Midwinter cheated.

EIGHT

Suddenly, it was to be a good summer. One morning, then two, then three dawned bright and glittered all day, spears of light on the water. Began to burn. The sea-sun was dangerous. Trippers bared their tripe-white bodies recklessly and fried a painful scarlet.

Suddenly, even though the schools had not yet broken up, the guest-houses and hotels were taking bookings for as far ahead as September, doing good business already. The town awoke, bustled. On the quay the scent of ozone mingled with that of frying chips and from the posh restaurant garlic, rich sauces. Foreign yachtsmen rowed or puttered to the quay or the club landing, stalked the streets of Poltrue like aliens from another planet, complained in the delicatessen. They were deeply tanned, exotic as migrating birds chattering of landfalls elsewhere. The dog warden patrolled Poltrue's small beach for sinners. Sheep-dogs yipped for sticks to be thrown. One morning there was a wonder: out of the morning mist there formed the spars of a three-master. She hung there between sea and sky, ghost-ship at the harbour mouth. Could I catch it? wondered Molly. But as she laid the wash on the paper the sun burned away the picture.

Something other than beauty was in the air.

Intemperance.

Poltreth was in a fever of illicit couplings. In a community so small incest smacked her lips, lust feasted, all the hungrier for the darkness of its winter. Gladys knew the names. When they were spoken of the end of her nose twitched. She had asked Tinker and he had made Hazel a bigger cage. Gladys put in a buck. For a week the two rabbits turned their backs on each other. Tinker said he reckoned Glad had been sold a pup. How do you sex a rabbit? Gladys said it would be all right, she'd had it from a friend.

(Gladys had many friends now. She seemed to be collecting both people and animals. To Selina and Sally and Sandra had been added, among others, Menhenniot, the Poltrue butcher. 'Not butcher,' said Gladys, who had been shown his knives at the back of the shop one Sunday. 'Meat Surgeon.')

The early morning after Hazel had woken them all screaming in the night, presumably at the loss of her virginity, Penny's Stan arrived on his motor-bike: a third-hand, converted Norton Commando.

'Would you like some coffee, Stan?' Molly said.

'Yuh.'

He seemed to Molly even more hirsute than ever. His eyebrows had practically joined his beard which in turn was tangled with his chest-fur. And so black. Could he be turning into an animal, she wondered distractedly. Then Tinker came down and the two giants thumped each other on the back.

'Hey, Stan, how's it going then?'

'Yuh.'

'I've got to go to school.' Jason surveyed his natural father with polite indifference.

Penny got up at midday and asked Molly if they had a black rubbish bag. Stan, tonight at least, would sleep on the beach. Meanwhile she took Stan back upstairs and Molly, washing the breakfast dishes, turned up the radio not to hear those frightful grunts interspersed with higher responses, not unlike Hazel's screams in the night. The twins, grinning and dribbling, seemed to like the noise.

'What's that? That cry?' Walter opened his eyes.

'Nothing. A gull. You were dreaming. Here's your coffee. Do you want the binoculars? There.'

It was three weeks now and Walter's back had failed to respond to her kneadings, to rest, to pills, even to Gladys's herbal brew. Tinker had fixed up a kind of day-bed in the shade from which Walter could watch the harbour. He raised the binoculars. There was Martha Price in halter top and shorts on her terrace. As Walter watched, she looked up from her gardening and smiled straight at him.

'Oh, I meant to say,' Molly called back as she set off down the hill. 'Martha's asked us all to the moor. Midsummer's Day.'

When the women were gathered on Martha's terrace, as they seemed to be lately about once a week, Walter would watch them through the binoculars. He wondered what they talked about. Gathered there, some in the shade, some with their faces turned to the sun, they struck him in their womanly postures as exotic, powerful even. The way they disposed themselves: resting, with heads bent over work, turning to speak to each other, standing, moving. The older woman straight-backed in a higher chair, wearing a wide straw hat, the others in deckchairs or on loungers, deferring to her, and she, in turn, to them. As the sun rose towards noon their limbs grew summer-heavy, their work was put aside or fell from their hands. A few would move into the shade behind the trailing vine. Then a tray would be brought out, glasses handed round.

Even their movements were beautiful: a hand reaching to touch another's arm, the other dipping her head towards the first, the cheek to cheek greeting that was both a kiss and a signal or salute between creatures of the same species.

Then one he recognised to be Martha stood and stretched, tall, bare-breasted, casting no shadow.

Walter put down the binoculars. He felt as though he had been spying on divinities at some ritual – ashamed.

Sally formerly of the dairy (in her seventh month of pregnancy by whom she knew not, she had given up work), yawned into the sun and piled her long, slightly dirty black locks on top of her head.

'Should I put it up?'

'Cooler,' Molly said. 'But not till I've finished this.'

She was painting Sally. That is she had begun a portrait shyly half a dozen times then snapped her Venus HB pencil in half and dashed straight into bold brushwork. Maybe acrylics were cheating but they dried so fast you got no second chance. Good. Her first attempts had stopped just below the breasts. Now she followed where the brush led to encompass the swollen slope of the belly under the thin shift. She was startled by the urge she had to touch that stretched mound, to let her hand rest there. The others felt the same, she suspected; there was a queer tingle today. In the end it was Sally's sister, Selina, who drained her wine and grinned.

'Go on, Sal, show them.'

They all looked round at Norah but she was dozing, her crochet in her lap.

'OK.' Sally shrugged, pulled up her skirt and Molly sat, her brush poised. She had forgotten the sheen to the drawn flesh, the veins, the navel. Penny in her pregnancies had looked like a gerbil that has swallowed a large tennis ball but Sally, lounging with her large feet planted apart, was formidable. No meek Henry Moore mother this. Her grinning, yellow-toothed expression was one of careless triumph with a hint of scorn.

Even Sandra, the bright little rat from the hairdressers, put down the brush and lacquer with which she had been shaping her hair into a bright purple crest.

'You can feel it moving.'

Selina, as skinny and blonde as her sister was dark, had her hand on the hump.

'Hey, lay off, Sill.'

'No. It's good luck. Like touching a hunchback. It's wriggling like a fish. Want a feel, Molly?'

Molly smiled and shook her head. She was aware, without looking round, that Martha, her long legs stretched out on the terrace wall, was watching her, amused. Watching the whole scene.

Why should something so ordinary – a condition women went to such lengths to avoid – hold the hypnotic power of a totem? Molly puzzled. But her brush was moving too fast for thought. She hardly noticed when Sally dropped her dress, yawned her farewell and the others too, left, Norah having missed the drama entirely ('Oh dear, has something happened? I must have been asleep'). When Martha came back from seeing the others out, Molly had changed the picture entirely, laying paint over paint. That extraordinary play of sea-light on Sally's skin as if she were an underwater creature. The heavy, waiting breasts. The elephant toes.

'Here.' Martha put down a mug of coffee.

'Thanks.' Molly realised she had been holding her breath. She tipped back her chair, astonished at what she had done. Since the first sketch Sally's head had retreated, so the hair seemed tangled with the trailing vine. From her shadowed, sturdy neck and shoulders grew the breasts – whorls of yellow ochre, fat, twin suns – then the pear-shaped body hardly recognisable as a body at all. Something blue-veined and pendulous from which there thrust that alarming and commanding circle. That O. And just above the forward-rounding of the O, not the curl of the navel but an eye. Indifferent. Bold. Outstaring.

'That's good, you know. Really good.'

Molly felt from behind Martha's hands on her shoulders.

'But you'd better put the brush in water before it dries out.'

'Yes.'

Molly's hand shook. She could hardly grasp the mug but was glad of the coffee.

'I don't understand.'

'Why d'you need to understand?'

'I don't know. I don't know why I painted it like that.'

I do, thought Martha. Who had lived too long. For ever. Seen the totem in a desert place, heard the shuffle of feet in the dancing circle. The song that came from the throat: umaywah-umm. The great O, the Oom. In Egypt spied upon a woman made barren by a hex, who caught the first warm blood from the beast, smeared breast and belly. Bore child.

'It doesn't matter why.'

Molly shook her head, still bewildered. Her first reaction had been astonishment. Then horror. What kind of person would paint such a thing? Now she looked again. Could Martha be right? Was it good? She turned away then glanced back as if to catch it unawares.

'Put it away,' Martha said. 'Don't look at it for a week.'

'Can I leave it here?'

'If you like. But it's yours. I'll keep it for you.'

The paint was dry already. Molly tore out the painting and

pushed the pad into her canvas bag, washed her brushes in
Martha's basement sink. As she walked up the hill towards
Jason's school she began to smile.

'You look funny, Granny.'

'Do I, darling?'

'No – all right funny, I mean.'

'Good.'

'You are thirteen then?'

Midwinter had got up to the terrace by the steep flight of
steps from the foreshore. Martha cursed herself. She'd locked
the street door shut but never thought of the beach way up. He
was sitting in the shade in Norah's chair, legs crossed. He had
done himself up in neo-colonial fashion: pale linen suit, panama
hat, white shoes. Immaculate.

Martha stood over him.

'No we are not. If you're looking for a coven you'll have to go
elsewhere. Try Morwena. Meanwhile, get out of my house.'

'Don't tell me it hasn't passed through your mind.'

'Even if it had I wouldn't do anything about it.'

'Reformed?'

'I never worked that way. You know that.'

'Perhaps I'll drop in some time.'

'All you would find is women who enjoy each other's company.
If you can understand that. We paint, sew, talk – that's all.
Though I fail to see what any of this has to do with you.'

'Everything you do concerns me.'

'If you're trying to seduce me –'

'Couldn't, my dear, if I tried. The Principessa is understand-
ing, bless her. No, I just don't care to see you wasting your
gifts.'

'Out!'

'Oh, very well. You always were scratchy, Martha. You should
watch that.' At the door Midwinter paused. 'You can't quite have
forgotten? I did please you once?'

As she bolted the door behind her Martha felt her cheeks
flame. She leaned against the door until her breath came evenly.
Midwinter impotent! Her own cracked laughter startled her.

Washing up, she broke a mug, grasped the edge of the sink. He could still shake her. And after all, what was she trying to make of herself? A woman of virtue? A harmless goodwife, like Judith pottering among her herbs?

Quite abruptly, Martha wished above all things that she could pray. But to whom?

NINE

Nature was putting on a harlot's show this summer. Even in the hinterland of ugly, wistful retirement cottages, gardens spilled over. Hosepipes were banned in this land of rain and washing-up water was saved for the evening ritual that kept the plants alive. Stan and Tinker between them rigged up a system by which bath water could be channelled, without heaving of buckets, through a plastic pipe to the vegetable garden.

Tess and Humph came down for a long weekend, Tess cross from the city. Tess said Walter's back was all in his mind. If he couldn't pull himself together he ought to be stretched.

For the grass there was not enough water. Norah and Gerald sat under a parasol on the parched lawn of the Channel Hotel. Gerald talked about Simla, quite coherently, then the blinds were drawn over his eyes. On the recommendation of the librarian, Norah was reading Barbara Pym. She explained to Gerald that once you had understood all the animals were people and the people animals, you knew, so to speak, where you were. Not that that was anywhere she particularly wanted to be.

Norah longed to be on the moor with the others but to leave Gerald for a whole day was unthinkable. It would have been tiring, after all, in this weather. She tried to imagine it but all she could see, as her own lids drooped, was spring in the hills of the Jordan valley, the dust flowering.

Later, in the cool of the evening, a whisper ran through the hotel: she's down, the Principessa, she has come down! She has left the Ocean Suite, she is being carried downstairs.

The Ocean Suite had its private lift, a marvellous affair, a golden cage with buttoned plum velvet seats, the entrance flanked by two bronzed, full-breasted nymphs bearing light fittings in the shape of flaming torches – all left over from the days of glory.

Norah, crossing the foyer on the way out to her evening constitutional, saw the Principessa's fragile bundle of bones in the arms of the sturdy handyman, carried from the lift – Midwinter and the manager attendant – out of the hotel and down the steps to the road level where she was laid most tenderly in, or rather upon, a kind of pram: a basket lounger padded with cushions and fitted with wheels and pushing handle. Norah slipped out of the side gate and across the road, so that she was standing, resting on the wall gazing apparently across the harbour and out to sea, at a point where the pram was bound to pass her.

As they came level, the Principessa, huddled in furs and scarves, gave no sign, but Midwinter inclined his head most politely and raised his panama. Such a handsome man and so well turned out (yet Martha seemed not to care for him at all). So pale though. And that burn mark: it looked almost as if he had covered it with talc, face-powder even. Poor man.

At the top of the hill – the incline grew less taxing once one was past the hotel – a thin hand in a lilac glove signalled stop. There was a kind of belvedere here – a half circle between the road and the cliff-fall where one could stand or sit (a famous place for lovers and suicides).

They became one of the sights that summer: Midwinter and the Principessa, taking the evening air.

For the drive to the moor they had worked out that Walter could lie flat in the back of the estate van while Penny would come with Stan on the motorbike (Tess was down and would have the twins) and Tinker would take in his van Gladys, Sally and Selina, with Martha going ahead alone to open up the cottage. At the last moment Jason announced that his snake was sick.

'He's gone in the compost heap and he won't let me stroke him.'

Molly bent to look. Not that there was anything to see but the tip of a tail.

'I expect he's hot, darling. It'll be cooler in there.'

'Can't we take him with us?'

'No, Jason. That would be cruel.'

'We're taking Enoch.'

'That's different.'

Martha had prepared a picnic outside the cottage, which at first sight appeared no more than a heap of stones huddled at the crossroads between hills and stream. The bumpy drive over the dry moor had been a torture for Walter, who sat now in the shade, his back against the dry-stone wall. If he kept very still the pain quietened. The slightest movement, even the raising of a glass to his lips, brought back the sensation that cruel knots had settled for ever each side of his lower spine. Perhaps Tess was right when she said his back was in his mind? Could lumbar distress be the manifestation of a soul in pain? Or was he simply a vertebrate who had failed to make it to the beach?

'Well?'

He opened his eyes. The others had eaten the tangy cheese, pâté, home-baked bread. He had drunk wine, taken a little soft cheese. Then they had scattered. Sally and Selina with Gladys hunting vervain and mugwort for the good-luck fire. Stan and Tinker, on the hill inside the stone circle, were digging a firebreak around the heaped wood. Molly, at the top of her life, wandered with Jason. He ran ahead, Enoch thumping at his heels, then waited for her to catch up. There was a flash of sea. Jason put his hand in hers. She thought: nothing can ever be better than this.

Martha, barefoot, wore a long, flame-coloured cotton shift and her hair loose. Her toe-nails were dirty, the palms of her feet calloused and hard. She looked down at Walter.

'You're awake then?'

'Yes. It's beautiful. I didn't know. Those stones –'

'Neolithic. Give you a guided tour some time. But there's something better. Stand up.'

'I can't.'

'Here.' She took his hands, his back protested, but he was standing. Martha grinned. 'One step for evolution. Now walk.'

Walter laughed painfully.

'It's absurd. I can't. Like a child learning.'

He longed to lie down flat on the ground but Martha seemed to be challenging him. She stood there, hands on hips. He remembered the top button of her shirt at their first proper meeting. Undone. Had that undone him? All this time, that state of anxious stasis, those dreams, frets, longings, intimations – was that what it all came down to? One button? He wanted Martha Price more than he had ever wanted anything in his life.

'Stand up straight,' Martha ordered. 'No, straighter. Now reach up with your arms. Stretch. Higher. Get away from the wall.'

A shade better. But the screws each side of his spine still threatened.

'Fine. Now walk. No, don't look at your feet. Take proper steps. It's on the flat then just a small climb. Stretch again if it helps.'

Martha led. Walter, arms up in an attitude of surrender, begging heaven, followed.

Molly and Jason were making their way to the highest point in the immediate field of vision, where flat rocks, like a Titan's cairn, were heaped one upon another. Distances, Molly soon discovered, were deceptive. Already they had walked half an hour and the hill seemed no nearer. She had sunk down thankfully onto the bare earth before she realised that the stone against which she rested was one of a circle. Not unlike the group near the cottage but taller. She could hear but not see a lark above, while below, the burned, featureless, near tree-less landscape fell away. That must be the cottage: in a squint in the folded hill she could see what might be a chimney and the arms of the dead tree leaning in pain away from the west. Though no wind blew today. Was that a mine-shaft over there or a rock that looked like a castle? A place full of traps, she supposed, in other weather, but today a wonderful emptiness.

Jason was running in a circle from stone to stone, touching each in turn. Enoch had started to follow him then given up and returned to pant by Molly.

'Hello, Enoch.' One thump of the tail. Wise dog.

'Granny! Why are the stones shining?'

'Something to do with the granite. I think it's called mica. Or there might be quartz.'

'Martha says they're magic.'

'I wouldn't be surprised.'

Nor would I, she thought. She laid her flaming cheek against the stone and it was cool. More than that? A tingle? A feeling they might speak, were speaking. Silly. When you don't know what something is for you can imagine it's anything.

With eyes half closed, she thought she could just make out figures on the mound by the cottage.

'Jason, sit down for a minute. You'll burn up. Look, isn't that Tinker? Where's Stan?'

'We're having a bonfire tonight.'

'Yes, I know.'

'What for?'

'Midsummer. They used to be afraid when the sun got lower, you see. So they tried to help it by lighting fires.'

What was that? Small hooves on hard ground. Molly was startled.

'Only a cow.' She heard its breath before she saw it and the animal appeared equally surprised. A young heifer that might have sprung from a cave-drawing of cattle: short in body and leg, something odd about the shape of its head. Horned. Patches of winter's furry coat, barrelled ribs. Grazing must be terrible in this weather. 'Come on then. If we're going to the top.'

Molly climbed now with her head down, her scarf covering the back of her neck. Jason had Stan's colouring, hardly needed his bush-hat. Molly thought of the ages this place encompassed, scanned the ground for fossils, flints, signs of man. Down there the pylons marched. Men had crawled under this earth after tin, gold. There was even a flower, slender and spiked with pale lilac flowers. It must be immensely strong though it seemed to her too fragile to survive.

Penny had dragged Stan away from his digging. She led him to a hollow – hardly more than a dent – in other weather it might have been a dewpond. She slipped off her cheesecloth skirt. She had found some pale flowers and stuck them in her hair. She pulled at Stan's belt, lay down and spread her legs.

'Vervain,' said Gladys.

'Get plenty.' Sally was sunning herself while Gladys and Selina hunted for the flowers of ritual. They had found a spot where a stream had at some time been dammed. It was hardly more than a trickle now but enough: a few thirsty plants hung onto life. 'And you'll need mugwort.'

'Is that it?' Gladys looked doubtful. 'How ugly.'

Selina came over to look.

'That's right. It never is very pretty but we're lucky to find it. It's an autumn flower really.'

Sally yawned. The heat had sucked the colour from the sky.

'Ought to have bones really for a foul fire.'

'What do you want a foul fire for?' Gladys was aware that she was getting on. But she hadn't learned anything yet, by half.

'Well, you know how hot weather makes you sexy.'

'I daresay.' Gladys thought of Menhenniot. He'd have had bones.

'So dragons copulate, don't they? And the stink drives them off.'

'Dragons!' Gladys snorted. Some of the stuff Sally and Selina had told her made sense – herbs and all that – but she hadn't made up her mind about the rest. The tricks they got up to. She had a pretty good idea what Martha Price was but it didn't seem to do her much good, did it? Didn't get you friends, that sort of thing.

Tempting, all the same, she reflected, as back in the cool of the cottage she put the kettle on. Not dragons and bones and nasty fires but doing what you wanted. Everything. Oh, yes, they'd have to take notice of Gladys then. All the world. Everyone.

'See!'

Martha stood at the top of the incline. For the last step, to pull him up, she reached for Walter's hand. There, in a lap of the moor, in the desert landscape, a blue eye winked.

'There's lots of them. Pools like this. Sometimes a disused quarry, sometimes a spring. You have to know where they are.'

'It's incredible.'

'Not really.'

But it was. Like a window through which you could see the waters of the earth. More precisely, cold-smelling, clean, tempting.

Martha had let go of his hand, pulled off her shirt and was already swimming. The finger that had once plucked him from the water now summoned him: 'Come on in.'

The first step was icy. Walter flapped his arms like a bird then he was out of his depth and Martha was gone. To reappear at his side, laughing. She splashed him and swam away. He followed. With the little heap of clothes on the bank he had shed so much.

'How's your back?'

'Can't feel it.'

But he could feel her legs circle his waist. He was just treading ground.

'Slowly,' she said. Then: 'Yes, like that.'

They lay, still in the cup of the pool, their lower limbs under water, wavering.

Walter dipped his face between her breasts.

'I dreamed about you. I dreamed you were a gull.'

'No – stay. Perhaps I was.' I was.

He was just as she had imagined: the pale limbs, long, unveined legs like a young man's.

Martha heard the drumming on the hard earth before he did and for a second she tensed (just Midwinter's style to spoil everything). The beat was too insistent for cattle. The shadow reached across the water to finger them. Martha smiled.

Epona. If so, the divinity was in poor shape – a half-starved mare in foal.

'Just a wild horse. I expect this is their pool. We've scared them. Listen. You can hear them running.'

'I want to see you.'

'No. Not there.'

He ran a finger along the scar, kissed it.

'It's ugly.'

'No. Nothing about you is ugly. You're perfect.'

She had her fingers in his grizzled hair and tugged quite hard until Walter had to look, to see her.

'You must never believe that. Never!' But she could not hold onto her will. She had done something she had sworn never to do and without tricks. How's that, Midwinter? No games.

All the same.

She could not resist.

'I could take you anywhere. I can show you everything,' she whispered. 'We can hide. We can change. We can be anything.'

'Mmn.'

Out of the water Walter knew how Adam felt. His nakedness was ashamed.

He could have sworn he heard a bark.

'Enoch – what's the matter?'

It should have been fresher at the top but instead Molly found she could hardly breathe. Jason was climbing the cairn. Enoch barked, once.

'Jason! Hurry up. We can't stay here. What can you see?'

'Everything.'

'Be careful.'

A clatter of stones and Jason was beside her. 'I could see the cottage and Tinker. And then I think it was a pond. A big one.'

'Surely not up here. Where?'

'There! Look.'

It could be. Something blue, like an O. No, a squashed O. An eye. Even as she watched a puff of cloud came up from nowhere, the eye blinked and shut.

Enoch, sure-footed, led the way down.

Tinker carried the brand that lit the fire.

Sally, rather than Martha, was the presiding goddess, supervising all from the baking of potatoes and the frying of sausages to the making of chaplets of vervain and mugwort.

'And as you leave you throw them in the fire,' Sally decreed.

'Why?' Gladys wanted to know. The truth was, she was a little squiffy from the wine. And not the only one.

'How the hell should I know?'

'For luck,' Martha whispered. She kept the mugs topped from litre bottles and coming upon Molly kissed her on the cheek.

'It's the colour of blood,' Molly said.

'Then blood it is,' said Martha and made a pass with her hand across the wine. She was in her fullness tonight, her great wickedness. She kissed the men full on the mouth. At the same time strove to bind the women to her, in sisterhood. A nod and Tinker plunged the brand into the kindling. A wink and Sally gave her deep-throated laugh.

The flames leaped up, the fat moon rose and Molly found Walter sitting cross-legged against a standing stone.

'Your back?'

'Better! Cured!'

Then why did he look sheepish? A silly grin she had never seen on his face before.

Oh well. Drink up.

'Your shirt's damp.'

'Must be the dew.'

Then someone – Sally perhaps – called: 'Now!'

Martha led, then all, even heavy Sally, joined hands and to Jason's triumphant thumping of the drum (empty oil-can) trod the ground in a circle within the circle round the fire, once, twice, thrice. Then Jason threw down the drum and joined them. They needed no music. They had the beat.

'The circle must not be broken!'

Who called?

Between Martha and Walter, Molly gasped. She had a queer taste in her mouth. She was dizzy with the flickering faces, like firebrands themselves. She made to break away but Martha squeezed her hand tighter. As the dance picked up speed the other circle, the stones within which they danced, seemed to grow taller, to sway, close in.

At the moment Molly felt she would fall, her head was spinning so, Martha let go her hand, the circle broke and, Selina leading, all flung into the fire the chaplets with which Sally had crowned them.

With the breaking of the circle the frenzy had left them yet as they gasped and laughed and prepared to go, there was the feeling that something had happened. They re-turned to themselves, their own natures, but the fire was still king and they were reluctant to abandon it. Even Molly lingered, unsure what she had seen and heard. Other fires? Voices?

Then Jason came up, too bright-eyed, kept up too late.

'I found Enoch. He was hiding. He didn't like the fire.'

'I expect he was frightened.'

'No. He wasn't frightened. He just didn't like the fire. Granny, I'm tired but I don't want to go to bed.'

Molly hugged him to her side.

'We must all go to bed.'

Martha locked up the cottage and they set out to leave, though not exactly in the order in which they had arrived. Selina sat on Tinker's lap, considerably endangering his driving. Walter rode with Martha. Enoch chose Molly's estate van.

Molly called: 'Stan, Penny, be careful. Follow Martha. She knows the way.'

Tinker had killed the fire with earth. It was cold now and a perilous journey to the moor gate unless, like Martha, you knew the traps and the tricks.

So the caravan set out, following Martha's tail-lights, from a small darkness to one which seemed this moonless night to stretch to the ends of the known earth.

TEN

Jason must have got up before dawn to dig his way into the centre of the compost heap.

'My snake's dying. Its insides are coming out.'

'Surely not, darling.'

Everyone else had slept late after the trip to the moor. Molly's dreams had been wild and she felt faintly sick. Sicker as she bent over to inspect the snake. The jelly-like excretions about an inch long looked moist. Jason's face was pale with exhaustion and distress, his eyes too bright.

'Gladys! Come and see my snake!'

Gladys appeared appallingly awake. She wore her new fuchsia stretch slacks, Max Factor pancake make-up and an air of indomitable complacency. It was hard to remember the mouse she had been.

'Eggs,' said Gladys.

'Eggs? How extraordinary. What do we do?'

The snake had puffed itself up and was hissing alarmingly.

'Cover her again. Leave her alone. They'll hatch in six weeks or so.'

However did Gladys know that? Molly wondered. But then why shouldn't she? Somehow they had all imagined she herself was hatched, pebble spectacles and all, in the Godalming Health Food shop where Walter had found her. But even Gladys had a history. It was simply that no one ever asked her about it and she never spoke. Once Molly would not have bothered. She was not sure now that she would dare.

Jason was cheered at the prospect of baby snakes. For the first week he had to be dissuaded from digging again to see how they were getting on. Suddenly noticing his grandson, Walter was very sweet with him. Then there were other things to do this glorious summer and Jason seemed to forget.

From time to time Molly remembered. That is, she would be picking beans in the small vegetable plot in the landward side of the house, giving the earth its daily drink of bathwater, throwing peelings onto the compost heap or simply resting, her mind empty, and the image would come to her of that dark nest.

All the same, she was content enough. Too busy to ask herself if she was content (wings like scissors, beaks like knives). People to feed. Tinker seemed in no hurry to return to his itinerant life. He took on odd jobs at the Poltreth boatyard and anywhere else he could find work. At the Poltrue Pine Workshoppe, then private carpentry-work too small for the local builders (he had a way with widows). For recreation he was helping with the carnival float at the Ferry Inn. Molly suspected there was a girl – he had taken to rowing over to Poltrue after supper and returning some time in the night long after the last ferry. That was normal enough, to be expected, and Molly wondered why she minded when she caught a glimpse of him in the Lugger with a girl whose bright but unwashed hair, raggedly trailing red skirt above bare feet and bracelet-encircled ankle she recognised.

'I can't think why I mind,' she confessed to Martha. With the coming of full summer the meetings of the women on Martha's terrace had been tacitly suspended but Molly still found herself drawn there. She would take a fresh-pulled lettuce to Norah and one for Martha on the way back. A couple of times she found the street door locked. Once at low water she came up from the beach.

Martha was looking well. No longer sallow but deeply tanned. Less jagged, angular. Not softer exactly but her eyes seemed larger. She had abandoned the shorts for a skirt, or rather, a sarong-like garment split at the side. She seemed just to have pulled it on.

'Sorry. Locked the door. I was sunbathing starkers. Why do you care that it's Selina?'

'I don't really, now I've said it.'

'They all look like sluts nowadays.' Martha studied Molly

speculatively through a cloud of smoke. 'That nonsense on the moor didn't get at you, did it? It was just fun.'

'Oh, no.'

'Good. How's the painting?'

'I haven't had much time. The children. Penny's Stan. Jason breaks up soon.'

I sound plaintive, Molly thought. The conversation we are having is not at all what we are talking about. She realised how much Martha's friendship meant to her. Perhaps too much? She had never had such ease with another woman as in the early days of that summer on this terrace. She closed her eyes against the sun.

'Martha, did you ever have any children?'

When she looked again Martha's expression had changed. She was sitting head dipped, her features winter-gaunt again.

'No. That is, just an abortion once.'

'I'm so sorry.'

Martha shook her head.

'No need. I was thankful.'

'I can let myself out,' Molly had said. On the way through the room to the street door she saw that Martha had hung her portrait of Sally above the day-bed. She stood in front of it then turned, certain for a mad moment that she was being watched.

'Oh, Pounce. You made me jump.'

The little cat was sitting on a high beam. It was funny how cats always seemed to be watching.

Stepping out into the dark side of the street, Molly sneezed.

Jason's school holidays started. Visitors took over Poltrue, both the waters and the town, so the locals who in other seasons would meet, pause to talk, shop companionably, now did their errands early while they could still move in the streets. Molly crossed rarely, only to supplement her shopping, sometimes to sit with Norah in the garden of the Channel Hotel, less and less to Martha's. In the comparative peace of Poltreth she moved, worked, sat, tranced, seeing as though from a great distance Walter setting off to the boat every morning like a man going to the office. Once or twice he asked Jason to join him but the boy seemed to prefer swimming to the idea of sailing. Just as well, perhaps. Walter looked relieved. His back had entirely healed and he seemed to have shed ten years. On the less crowded beach to the east she sat, her sketch pad untouched beside her, waved at Jason, or at his shadow-shape, playing in the sea. Or it might have been another child. When, stunned by the midday heat, she shut her eyes, that was what she heard – above the sea, the gulls disputing territory, the yelp of the water-ski boat: the children's summer cries.

This was the beach that lay at the foot of the precipitous path where Walter had fallen. Or, rather, down the path – skirting the one where the dredger dumped every day and only trippers swam – and when the tide was out, round the rocks. At other times, a dog-leg to be taken halfway down that same path: a longer walk but a kinder descent.

This was the beach where Stan and Penny slept. Jason was still lofty with his natural father. Stan picked up his twins gently and in wonder, one in each hand. Molly could have sworn he was sniffing them.

Women brought the children here. The women sat on the beach. There was an invisible connection, a nervous system fine as a web between the women with their beach-bags, sun-oils, books, towels, picnic boxes, flasks. From a gull's eye view they had the appearance of statues of sand. Then there would be a twitch on the thread that ran between them and the playing children and one statue would stand, covering her eyes against the sun, searching out her child in the water. At a certain time of day their standing shadows reached across the sands, fingering the sea's edge for their children.

The cliffs were dangerous. So was the strong tide on the ebb. There were accidents, rescues, but no fatalities. One maroon was fired for the coastguard, two for the lifeboat. Then the child who had gone out too far or climbed too high was scooped up.

The beach returned to itself. The women to their dreams.

In sleep Molly waded through rising waters but they had the thickness of fur. She felt a hairy pelt like Stan's brush her thighs and the sea-serpents mouthing. Floating on the surface, Walter's grey locks were seaweed, his eyes empty circles of bone. The seagulls cried with the voices of children.

'Granny! Wake up. You're dreaming.'

'Jason?'

'You made a funny noise.'

'Sorry, love. Come on, it's cold. Time to go home.'

Walter roared, growled, he was king. Then Martha bit him, laughed, flung him off. He chased her into the water. He knelt beside her day-bed and nibbled her toes. He adored her. He had had such worship in him. She was Nut. She reached across the arc of the earth from sunset to dawn. She made herself small, curled, the whorl of a shell. He could have sworn one night she was a cat. He loved the dry skin on the soles of her feet, round her toes, her smoky kiss. Stained fingers. Teeth. Nubbly belly-slash.

Enoch, stiff-backed, waited for him at the top of the cliff or at Martha's door: his conscience, disapproving. The new Walter – or the old one at last awakened – ignored him. The dog gave up his vigil, went back to pant in the shade of the water-butt. Martha's cat watched him go.

There was still the eye in that peculiar painting above the day-bed.

Walter motored out to the secret cove to the west. No Martha today. She was on her terrace, raised a hand as he passed. Then she was there, on the beach, spread like a seal on a warm, flat rock.

'But I saw you.'

'Well, I'm here, aren't I?'

'Oh. Yes.'

'Never heard of bilocation, have you?'

Watch it. You'll scare him off. But, oh, some tricks were irresistible! To creep into his bed at night while Molly slept on the other side. He'll think it's a dream. Martha no longer cared if Midwinter had the last laugh. She too was abandoned. Utterly.

At the same time she began to be afraid. Walter was a man made for guilt. When it struck him she would have to be ready but she had no idea what she would do.

And even in herself there were intimations, pricks of unfamiliar feelings. Hard to put a name on them.

Something like the first signs of flu – was that shame? The hint of a longing she could not identify to put away all tricks and live in the open, in the messy, ordinary world from which her nature shut her out, from which she had been glad to be excluded. (Poor fools, she always used to agree with Morwena, what hell!) One morning in the mirror that had never reflected anything but the room behind her, Martha thought for a second she caught the shadow of a cheekbone. It gave her both a scare and a thrill. If she hadn't known better, she might have said she was becoming human.

For several days Martha avoided everyone, including Walter. She pulled down her blinds and neither ate nor slept. She hung a cloth over the mirror. Pounce the cat watched her as she paced the big room, took the Fenny Trevanion papers, almost tore them up, then read on, that last sentence of Richard Rashlay's witness: I pray only that the Lord heard me and took her Soul to Him, for only in repentance may Sorcerers save their Souls.

'Balls!' Martha said, crumpling the paper for Pounce to play with. And what when they find out there is no Him? No soul? The sadness of witches is without end.

In this state she could normally leave her body with the greatest of ease. But for once escape was denied her.

What she needed was something to eat and Morwena's sharp tongue.

The moment she plugged in the telephone, it rang.

'Martha, darling, I wish you wouldn't do that.'

Martha sank down on the day-bed. Reached for a cigarette.

'Morwena.'

'Of course. Martha, I wish you wouldn't cut yourself off like this. You're not a naughty child any more and I've been worried half out of my mind. I nearly came over but what with Godfrey and all this business. I've been having some very peculiar vibrations about you. Maybe I'll come anyway.'

Martha smiled for the first time in three days.

'What about Godfrey? Godfrey who?'

'Your archivist baldy, of course. A nervous breakdown. I've put him in the Mayo Clinic and washed my hands.'

'I told you. You should never have taken him in the first place.'

'Martha, dear, I hate to say it, but could that be the pot calling the kettle black?'

'Thanks, Morwena.'

'What for?'

'Making me laugh.'

Oh, Lord, thought Martha, leaning back, you're not there, I know, but thank heaven for laughter. Come on, Pounce, let's have a blow-out. Herring heads and fried eggs and beans and jam. Smoked salmon for you. She flipped up the blinds.

Everyone said it was the heat. A people deprived of the consoling liturgy concerning the awfulness of the British summer, the plaint that kept them all sober and joined in a common sense of attrition, began to behave quite strangely, according to their natures.

Gerald thought he was young again and attempted to make love to Norah. In the middle of the night she woke to find him in her bed, naked, his body pressed against hers as he fumbled with her nightie buttons.

'Gerald! Please.'

'That's my girl.'

He abandoned the fumbling assault on her buttons, pushed her nightgown up and, panting with the effort, heaved his body until he lay on top of her.

'My girlie. My sweet girlie.'

After her first attempt to push him away, Norah lay very still. Her thought was, if he should die – his breathing was alarming – and I could not move him. He had always been a heavy man and nowadays, since the illness, heavier. If she put her arms round his back she might be able to budge him.

'Girlie loves me?'

Norah let out her breath. Now at least he was beside her rather than on top. She still had her arms round him though. It was unbearably hot but she kept them there. How long was it, how many months, years, since they had exchanged more than a kiss? Hardly even that lately. The feel of his flesh against hers like this was extraordinary and at the same time so familiar.

'Of course I do, my darling.'

She lay for a while until he slept then slipped her arm from under Gerald's shoulders and spent the rest of the night in his bed. When she lay down she found she was shaking and close to tears.

The weather brought a fleet of Portuguese men-of-war every afternoon to the swimming beach. The women would call the children from the water the moment they saw the tide turn or felt the onshore sea-breeze get up. There were rumours of sharks and stranger beasts than that.

Gladys announced she had given up vegetarianism. Menhenniot the meat surgeon had converted her. She was now a carnivore and rarely returned without a nice cut of pork or a bleeding bundle of offal.

Perhaps it was the heat. Possibly the offal would have been enough on its own. In either case, there was an odd little row.

Walter, who never knew what or if he ate, pushed his plate aside. Molly noticed but said nothing until she was washing up and Walter was drinking coffee by the open door. Tess and Humph, down for the holiday, sat on the grass a few yards away but they were regarding the view. Tinker, Stan and Penny had gulped their food and left. Gladys had gone wherever Gladys went these days.

Molly banged down the saucepan.

'There was nothing at all the matter with the liver. It was very good liver.'

Walter looked up, as startled as if Molly had turned into a tiger.

'You realise you've hurt Gladys?'

'I don't think Gladys minded.'

'What would you know about what anyone felt? You never have. You are the most profoundly selfish man I know.'

Walter looked as if he had been slapped. Molly burst into tears. Walter stood, helpless. For the first time in weeks his back twinged. Martha had been right about Walter. He was made for guilt. He called up Enoch and in the relative cool of the evening walked the cliffs, his conscience at his heels.

Molly flung the saucepan on the floor, imagined breaking. Everything. Plates, pots, dishes, knives, flying all flying, glass, glasses, windows, smashing into dangerous shards, cutting flesh, drawing blood. In her vision of the mad kitchen she stood sobbing, her hands over her eyes.

What?

'And what was all that about?' Humph, the mender, his arms round her shoulders, easing her into a chair, offering large, clean, white handkerchief.

'Humph? I don't know.'

They went as a family on the promised outing to Gwancarrek: Molly, Jason and Walter in *Cleo*, the others in Tinker's borrowed launch. They had an hour each side of low-water spring tide. They sat on the rock and ate Gladys's pickled beef sandwiches, courtesy of Menhenniot. A helicopter circled overhead like an attendant hornet. Someone had been swept out to sea last night and a new bride wept on the beach. There would be a body.

Walter sat on the rock with a handkerchief knotted at the corners over his head, his long legs drawn up under his chin. Ever since the outburst he had been windy of Molly. Surely if she knew about Martha, she would have said? Directness was Molly's way. After all these years she was still the most uncomplicated person he had known in his life. He sighed. The points of light on the water were blinding.

After the three days in which Martha's door had been locked and the blinds pulled down, she had emerged as though nothing had happened, looking thin and sallow. They had gone to the moor for the day, Martha driving, he thought, recklessly. He imagined they were going to the cottage but they were not. Instead, she flung the Land-Rover off the road, slammed on the brakes and led him across the moor to a hill crowned by large, flat stones. The sun up here was even more pitiless than on the ocean. This must be the highest point he guessed, for the land fell away endlessly. The landscape, parched even more since the day of the bonfire, was featureless, faintly alarming.

Martha smoked, screwed up her eyes, ground out her cigarette and piled earth on the butt.

'We're inhuman,' she said. 'You and I'

Walter blinked. He wanted to touch her, to lay his head in her lap but she was forbidding.

'I love you.'

'What I mean is, we don't feel properly, either of us. I'm not even sure I want to. I'm not calling it off. All I'm saying is that it could be dangerous.'

She kissed him once, firmly, on the lips. 'So think about it.'

'There's nothing to think.'

On the way back to the road, walking with his gaze downcast, Walter kicked up a stone. The earth had dried to sand, like the beach it might once have been. He turned the find idly in his hand, then looked closer. Extraordinary. The delicate tracings of creatures from an ancient sea.

'What's that?' Martha peered. She could have shown him. They could have stood hand in hand on that very beach. Oh, the temptation! Take my hand – we can leap up, look down on the very start of things!

Instead she nodded.

'The nice thing about evolution is that it is entirely without morality. Don't you think?'

Walter chewed this over like an old dog with a bone. He didn't know what to say. He never knew what to say when Martha was in this kind of mood. She spoke of serious things as if she were laughing in his face. All he could think at the moment was that he could not give her up. But no one must be hurt. Was that what she was trying to say? Someone will be hurt?

All he could manage for the time, in this heat and this bewilderment, was to put one foot in front of the other. He felt vertiginously aware of the casual laws of nature that pinned him to the ground and allowed him not only to stand but to move, against 40lb of pressure, through invisible waves of aether, on this wildly spinning planet. He slipped the fossil in his pocket and concentrated on keeping his balance.

Sitting on the rock, Walter fingered the fossil in his pocket. Molly was trying to paint the view but Walter kept getting in the way. Norah had lent her *To the Lighthouse* and she realised she had misremembered it. It was Lily Briscoe who did the painting and had the vision. Mrs Ramsay knitted. For the lighthouse keeper's son. Socks. A sock. There was something faintly irritating about Mrs Ramsay. Had Molly felt that on first reading? She thought not. The other thing she had forgotten about the book (or been incapable of perceiving all those years ago) was its capacity to alarm. All those beautiful words, you were lulled, your senses basked, then abruptly a tear in the curtain, a sense of danger, of a warning croaked offstage. Perhaps it was her own mood.

If only, like Lily, she could draw a line across the paper and say, well, that's that, it's finished. Novelists were lucky. They could hand over their visions and walk away, out of the picture. (With stones in their cardigan pockets to drown themselves.) Molly had just decided that if Walter were there she might as well put him in the picture. She had made the first brush-strokes when he moved.

'Walter?' she said, then suddenly saw what he was looking at, why he had stood.

A beautifully preserved or converted little steam-boat was making its way out of the harbour. Beneath the green awning the Principessa lay against heaped cushions, a rug across her legs, her face veiled and crowned by a wide, soft straw hat. A boatman was at the wheel. On the other side Midwinter sat, very still, very straight. Under the panama his face looked sea-green. His white linen trousers were immaculately pressed, his legs crossed. He smoked a thin black cigar and as the vessel chugged sedately past Gwancarrek, he put his hand to his panama and made a sketch of raising it, in polite salute.

Selina, sporting in the water with Tinker, giggled.

'Oh, look,' Gladys said. 'It's that nice friend of Mrs Price's. Mr Midwinter.' She took off her own floppy pink sun-hat and waved it.

As the steam-boat continued on its cautious tour of the ocean the sudden afternoon sea-breeze came up from the south. The face of the sea was hardly ruffled but Gladys's sun-hat was greedily snatched, as was Molly's painting.

Tinker churned the water in the smooth wake of the steam-boat. He waved something pink: Gladys's terrible hat.

'There you are, Glad. Got it! Ma? D'you want your painting? Bit wet, I'm afraid.'

Molly shook her head. She would never have finished it.

'Let it go.'

ELEVEN

At Poltrue, Carnival was in the air. The streets were in the process of metamorphosis into tunnels of greenery. Stan and Tinker helped at both Poltreth and Poltrue with the fixing of bunting, the strings of lights from roof to roof. More soberly, in the club committee room, plans for the Regatta were finalised.

Banished from their secret beach – no secret at all, really – Martha and Walter went far out to sea and made love precariously in the arms of *Cleo*. Fell in the water. Walter believed himself to be drowning, sank submissively, his grey locks trailing upwards, his eyes wide open in wonder or surprise. Martha saved him effortlessly, with one hand she brought him to the surface. He spat salt. She cradled him. She could never give him up. Ever. A porpoise jumped and laughed at them. When Molly did the laundry she found seaweed in his pockets.

The weather had begun to grumble at the heat. No storm yet but green flashes a hundred miles away on the north coast of France became a kind of firework show.

Molly sat sewing Jason's caterpillar suit for the Ferry Inn entry.

She snapped a thread with her teeth and Tess said: 'You do realise, don't you?'

'What?'

'He's having an affair. Walter. He's positively furtive.'

Molly watched Tess talk, her mouth moving, making indignant shapes. Her unpowdered nose was peeling for the second time. Round her advising mouth there was a web of small lines

that would settle, one day the wind changed, to sourness.
'I know.'

Molly tidied away her sewing. She checked the twins, put a
casserole in the oven and left a note for Gladys. She washed
her face, brushed her hair, pinned it up, put her purse in her
pocket and, leaving Tess by the water-butt, made her way down
the hill to the ferry. She looked over her shoulder once.
'No, Enoch. Go home.'
The old dog watched her all the same until she was safely on
the ferry. He stood, uttered a small whimper and regretfully
started the pad back home.

While Molly knocked, found Martha's door locked against her,
Martha was sitting in the Tower Suite of the Channel Hotel.
'Well, my dear, what a surprise!'
Midwinter was wearing a silk striped dressing-gown and
velvet slippers. He had been slow in answering and Martha had
nearly gone away.
'If I'm disturbing you –'
'Just a rest. But I was getting up. One does find this weather
amazingly tiring.'
Martha took him in. The burn-stain had nearly faded but
there was something insubstantial about him. His hands, as he
gestured to a chair, looked papery. His throat was corded like
an old man's. His lips were too pink, his hair too black, against
a face even more ashen than usual. There was a sickly smell,
as of some rotting plant. It was hard to believe that she had
ever been his handmaiden, however briefly.
'You look awful.'
Midwinter had seated himself tenderly, with his back to the
light.
'No need to growl, Martha. You came of your own free will.
And do stop ranging about like that. That's better. And stop
chewing your fingernails. There are cigarettes in the box there.'
Martha glowered.
'There's something I want to ask you.'
'Then ask.'

'But I'm not prepared to pay.'

Midwinter winced. His expression was of innocence affronted.

'Whenever have I asked you for anything?'

'You put me through the worst hell I've known. And don't tell me it was an accident.'

'Ah. Well. My regrets. May we get to the point? Something to do with your latest little folly, no doubt.'

'How do you know?' Stupid question.

'I keep an eye on you. I have concern for you.'

Martha bit her lip. Under the dressing-gown the line of his shanks was skinny. She took a deep breath.

'I want to know if I can change my nature.'

'Whyever would you want to do that?'

'I'm afraid of it.'

'In your present circumstances I'd be grateful. It gives you the upper hand.'

Martha could not sit. She paced to the tower window. There were three panes, one gave onto the river, one the harbour, the other the sea. She stood with her back to Midwinter. There was Molly at Martha's own front door.

'You haven't answered my question.'

'I think you know the answer already. You are your nature.' Midwinter's expression was weary, almost tender. He held up his hands and lowered them. For the moment at least, he seemed to have put aside his waspishness. Another trick, no doubt. Now he reached for his silver-topped cane, heaved himself with apparent difficulty from his chair and crossed the room to stand with Martha by the window. Below, the holiday-makers' small hired motor-craft screamed like buzz-saws, setting becalmed racing dinghies wildly lurching. On the small, filthy beach inside the harbour children whined, querulous with sun and exhaustion. A bent figure was making a crabwise passage up the Promenade towards the hotel. The widows' walk.

'You really want that? To be one of them?'

Martha shook her head.

'Lately I've wondered.'

She felt his hand on the back of her neck, his breath on her cheek. She had never accustomed herself to that stench.

'The wife knows about it,' Midwinter said. 'Pathetic. They live as long as flies and in such pain.'

'You have visitors.'

Sally, Selina and Sandra were climbing the steps to the hotel, Sally, vast now in her fullness, towed by the other two, all laughing. Sandra's hair looked like a parrot's plume. She wore a scatter of purple sequins and not much else.

Martha raised her eyebrows.

'Playmates?'

'If you would stay I can get rid of them. Look!'

As Midwinter spoke the whole scene froze. The girls were turned to statues, the busy harbour stilled, even the sun arrested on its downward arc.

'That old trick.'

'Wait.'

As she made to go, Midwinter called her back. He was scrabbling with swollen, white fingers in an ebony box by his chair.

'Here. Stand still for just one moment. Indulge me. One small present of no account.'

Martha stood, felt him slip the necklace over her head and round her throat. She looked down. A greenish stone.

'What is it?'

'Serpentine.'

'You're a fool, Midwinter. You're losing your touch.'

Almost, she felt sorry for him, as she stood at the door and saw him in his decay, the fluttering hand that would not be stilled, the pallor, the spindly ankles jutting from his robe, the painted lips.

'We had some times, though? Eh? You and I?'

On the way back the will had suddenly gone out of Molly, as if someone had snatched it away. If Martha had been in, she could not imagine what she would have said to her. She avoided Tess, watched Walter sleeping beside her and remembered that strange dream she had had when they first arrived: that he had been ensorcelled.

Tonight he had come home wearing the sheepish gaze of a

penitent, bringing her a bucketful of shining mackerel. He had even attempted to gut them himself until Molly took the knife from him. His sweater and trousers were covered in sticky scales.

'You look like a fish,' Molly said.

She smiled, holding the knife. Since the day she had gone for him so suddenly, they had both been wary, formal with one another, over-polite.

Walter opened his mouth and closed it. He went for a walk on the cliffs. When called, Enoch looked up but declined the invitation. Walter felt absurdly hurt.

Whenever Walter walked the cliffs gulls screamed after him for the bread crusts he carried always in his pockets. Tonight he had forgotten. The gulls cursed him, screeched in his wake.

Selfish, Molly had said, you think of no one but yourself. The truth was, Walter decided, most of his life he had had no sense of self. For a short time he existed when he thought God saw him. And with Martha? He had worshipped. He was her acolyte, simply. If she asked for his soul he would have handed it over – had he known where to find it. With her he forgot his loneliness in the world for she, he sensed, was the same. We are inhuman, she said. Was that what she meant? They were together outside the bright house of life?

Yet there was Molly. As dusk fell he could see her through the window, inside, moving around, lighting a lamp, holding out a hand to him. All he had to do was to take it, to go in.

While the staid Regatta was conducted on the water, a rocket announced the start of Carnival. Days and nights of barely controlled frenzy: of silver bands, dancing in the streets, on the quay. Fierce, horned figures, striding from pub to pub, thumping out on makeshift drums the call to chaos. Lashed their wicked tails, crossed to Poltreth and back on a raft, let off red smoke. Their forks of hell threatened the clogged crowds. The small fairy queen with attendants, so pretty and stiff on her float, was soon forgotten. There was a darker, more dangerous summons.

Stan clapped his hands together, Penny hung on his arm, dragged him into the graveyard, lay down.

Up at the Channel Hotel Molly had long ago seen Jason dance away with all the flurry dancers in his caterpillar suit. In the dusk she had sat with Norah on the lawn, watching the devils prance past.

A figure, resting with his hand on a stick, stood a little above them, higher up the lawn.

'Isn't that whatsis-name? Midwinter?'

(The Principessa lay in her suite, blinds and curtains drawn, ears stuffed with wax, black mask across her eyes.)

Norah said suddenly: 'We've been given notice.'

'Notice?'

'To get out. Gerald struck one of the waiters last night. He said he was the devil. The liver was poisoned. So he hit him. I knew it was coming, the violent stage, but I hoped he'd go first.'

'Oh, I am sorry. So sorry.'

A flare lit up the harbour. It died, leaving the darkness darker. Molly knew she must make her way down to the quay to collect Jason.

Norah said: 'I think life is terrible. Terrible and cruel.'

Martha sat hunched on the daybed, smoking.

'It's Molly, isn't it?'

Walter nodded.

'I don't know what to do. What we can do.'

'We'll have to see, won't we.'

'That picture –' Walter said.

'I hate the damn thing.'

When Walter had gone (a soul in torment), Martha sat for a while. Then she surveyed Molly's painting, tacked to the wall. While her little cat watched, she took up her scissors, hesitated, then stabbed them into the eye.

Sally, queening it on the dairy float, with Selina and Sandra attendant, yelled with glee.

Her waters had broken.

She tossed paper flowers each time she saw a lover.

And kisses. And winks.

'Here, give us the scrumpy,' she shouted, her crown of

Bacofoil tipped over one eye, her robes quite shamefully adrift, spilling out one bosom. 'I'm going to pop!'

The horizon flashed green. Across the moon a small messenger cloud announced a change in the weather. No rain fell, the storm was still sixty miles to the south but the air had been sucked from the hunched town.

Molly gulped for breath and plunged down the hill but soon ran into the cheery gang from hell doing their second round before they refuelled at the Compass Rose and set off for another circuit.

The St John's ambulance pressed from behind, the friendly fiends from in front. Between the two Molly struggled to keep her balance. She must be close to Martha's doorway, she guessed. At that moment she felt a sharp stab in one eye, as if she had been pricked.

As the first drop of warm rain fell, the baby snakes in the compost heap bit at their shells with their egg-teeth, popped out their wondering heads and withdrew.

Molly put her hand to her eye and sneezed.

Sally roared with her first contraction.

Midwinter in his tower pulled the curtains, yawned and went to bed.

ALL HALLOWS

TWELVE

The autumn rooks discussed winter. Molly heard their caw from her bed. The summer cold that started the night of Carnival had turned to fever and now a racking cough.

'What's that?'

'Brandy and lovage,' Gladys said. 'Then a nice bit of tripe.'

Molly declined the tripe, accepted the drink.

'How long have I been ill now?'

'A couple of weeks.'

'So long?'

When her temperature was at its highest, Molly had been adrift on a raft on a dark sea. There had been visitors. Gladys with her meat surgeon rowed past and Gladys waved her pink sun-hat. Martha, her hair flying, her cat on her shoulder, rode the wave that threatened to swamp the raft but never quite broke. Norah was beside her, staring straight ahead. Terrible, she said, cruel. Terrible and cruel. Molly woke crying.

'Walter!'

His face loomed.

'I thought you were drowned.'

'Now. Hush.'

Fighting someone – Gladys? Tess? Penny? – who pulled up the sheet Molly struggled to throw off.

'What's she saying?'

'Dreaming. She's only dreaming.'

Then she had woken properly, alone, feeling cold. The room was grey. Rain streamed down the window. Where had the summer gone?

She slept again. When she next opened her eyes Gladys was

sitting steel-backed straight by the bed, knitting something violently purple.

'Terrible storm the night of the Carnival,' Gladys said. 'That's when the weather broke. Tess has gone back to London. Good riddance. Sally had a nice big baby. Ten pounds.'

Molly closed her eyes against the flashing needles. She would have liked to close her ears.

'Walter? Sorry, I must have dozed.'

'You're better.'

'Much better.'

He stood between the door and the bed, his head ducked not to crack his skull.

'Oh. Good.'

He looked so hangdog Molly nearly laughed.

'I wasn't dying, you know. Just a summer cold.'

'That's right. You'll be up soon. Just a cold.'

He edged out backwards.

Only it wasn't funny, was it, Molly remembered. About Walter.

Time to get up.

The weather alternated, one day crisp, the next filthy.

Molly drank Gladys's potions, some, like the brandy and lovage, delicious; others foul. She stepped out at last into one of those tremulous, beautiful days, when the advancing autumn paused, the light smiled. A shower of gold hung on the trees but had not yet fallen.

She was so much better. All that bothered her still was a feeling in her eye, like a piece of grit. She bathed it and had to remember not to rub it.

Penny and Stan had gone off to the moor. To pick magic mushrooms? To procreate? They took two dozen black plastic dustbin liners, one blanket, a quantity of tinned food and Penny's own Walkman head-phones and ghetto-blaster. Surprisingly little, really but then Stan's huge motor-bike, hung with flasks and panniers and knives and tin-openers, was as much a ship of the desert as a camel. They left behind Penny's weirdly wandering knitting and the twins.

At least, Penny had weaned the twins before she left and Gladys, with the help of Enoch, took them over. She marched them down to the ferry in the double collapsible pram, showed them off all through the town, knitted garments in strange colours, gave them a nip of something when they squealed. She talked to them. What was she telling them? Stories? Sitting up now, they lurched over their safety harnesses, wide-eyed, dribbling with pleasure as Gladys talked. On half-day closing in the room behind the shop they watched Menhenniot flash his knives. They crowed. 'Ever so good,' said Gladys. 'Poor little things,' said Sally, bouncing her giant baby on her lap, 'let me give them a suckle.'

Molly hung on Tinker's arm.

'My snake died,' Jason said. 'It had a virus in its tail.'

'Oh, darling, I'm sorry.'

'It doesn't matter. I'm going to get a tortoise. I wanted a tortoise anyway.'

Molly could walk by herself. Round the house. A hundred yards along the cliffs. Down the small garden to inspect Jason's tortoise. He picked it up. It retracted its rather unpleasant neck and the head with the beak-like mouth.

'They get ticks,' Jason said. 'But you mustn't pull them out, you have to kill them.'

'How?'

'I don't know. I'm going to ask Gladys.'

'Where's the other rabbit?'

'Hazel bit it. Menhenniot said they were both bucks so he took it away. Menhenniot knows how to sex rabbits.'

Jason chattered on. Molly wondered what had happened to the young snakes.

'Why are you crying, Granny?'

'I'm not. Just something in my eye.'

Molly had not exactly forgotten the night of the Carnival. Why she had gone to Martha's. She would have to face Martha and Walter, to deal with it, to face it herself. Just for the moment though she would let it slide. Mentally, she still felt convalescent.

The odd thing was that although she should hate her, she

missed Martha. More than once she had to repress an absurd impulse to telephone her.

A couple came from a holistic commune inland to pay their respects to Walter, former father of the Earthfolk, and Molly watched, amused. If Walter had known how charming he was he would have charmed no one. His tentative, unfinished remarks, his half-smile, the way he had of nodding and rocking then suddenly unlocking his knees from his chin to fetch something or simply to make a point, his air of gentle wisdom, mild simplicity, enchanted the two visitors who returned the next day in the rain to lay at his feet pots of organic honey in tribute.

Tess rang from London.

'Well?'

'Well what?'

'Molly you're impossible. Have you said anything? To Walter? About that woman? Is it still going on?' Molly played with the telephone cord. 'Molly, are you there? Can you talk? Is Walter with you?'

'Yes. No. I mean, Walter's not here. Sorry, Tess.'

'What? I can't hear you. This line's terrible.'

Molly laid the telephone back in its cradle.

There was a gale. The Poltreth telephones were out of order. Molly sighed, made soup, looked out across the water. The skies had never been so wonderful.

Martha knew she had fudged it. She did not need Morwena to tell her so.

'You're just playing around.'

'She was quite ill. The trouble was that only made him feel more guilty.'

'She's alive, isn't she? And you want him?'

'Oh yes. I want him.'

'Well then.'

As soon as Martha had put down the telephone it rang again.

'Judith? Is that you?'

Judith always whispered at telephones, as though she feared they might go off in her face.

'Martha, darling, I've been so worried. I've had feelings. I couldn't sleep. Martha, you wouldn't do anything really wicked, would you?'

'I don't know, Judith. I truly don't know.'

Martha groaned. She picked up the telephone and flung it across the room. Pounce humped his back and opened his mouth at her in a soundless mew of disapproval.

Martha dismissed Walter, for the moment.

'We both need time to think. Molly knows.'

'Does she?'

Walter was both startled and lost. He could not bring himself to speak to Molly. He could not understand why she did not speak. It struck him that, except for Molly, he had no friends. Oh, he had rubbed along well enough with Humph Allgood but there was no one – but Molly – to whom he could bring anxiety, grief, unanswerable questions. There never had been, all his life.

The autumn trailed on: warm, damp weather broken only by gales, roaring in from the west. On the rare bright, still days, you could stand outside the cottage and see the smaller clouds, the forerunners, and close behind them the black front massing that would snatch leaves from trees, roofs from houses, children from sleep, souls from bodies. It left wrecks, floods, so much broken, lost, then bustled off eastwards satisfied, as though it had chosen this western land for special punishment.

Walter went out in *Cleo* in wild seas but he could not drown. Even running dangerously under bare poles with gale and sea, he survived. Had someone twitched a thread, pulled him back? He tugged harder, found he was yelling, singing as a black wave mounted. There were times like this when he would have chosen to die. On land, he walked to the churchyard, vaguely hoping to bump into Martha, found himself on the edge of a fresh-dug grave, looking down, in.

The bell scattered the rooks. They complained, returned, were scattered again as the funeral party made its way out of the church. The vicar was the good host speeding his guests. The mourners remembered weddings as the wind plucked at Norah's veil. Almost, she expected to hook her arm in her husband's but the bell said no. Thank you, she kept saying, thank you, and from the corner of her eye saw a cloaked figure turn the corner down the hill into Fore Street.

'I'm so sorry.'

Gerald Carteret was dead.

'Sorry.'

'Thank you.'

Molly kissed Norah's dry cheek, then left. This was the first time she had crossed to Poltrue since her illness. She pressed Norah's hand then made her way to the ferry. Was that Martha she had seen walking quickly before the wind? The ferry bucked. Spray was flung in her face. Between waves she caught a glimpse of Martha's pointed roof.

She was glad to be, for the length of the crossing, between shores, sorry when they had to land. There was the feeling that this time was no more than a pause.

Martha had never before in this life sought out her own kind. Yet here she was in the fuggy room behind the Lobster Pot watching Selina sort Hallowe'en masks.

The three – Sally, Selina and Sandra – had simply looked up and nodded when she tapped on the door and went in. Sally shoved Sandra who made room for Martha by the stove.

'Sill's helping out at the Treasure Chest.'

Sally put on a pig's mask, wagged her head at her huge baby. The baby roared and pulled her snout. Martha accepted a tin mug of black tea. Sally's marmalade cat with a bruiser's face and savagely chewed ears jumped onto Martha's lap.

There had been no need to explain. They knew.

Sally dumped the baby back in its battered cradle.

'Well then. If you want him you'll have to deal with her. From what I hear I'd say she's ripe. Scared. That's as good as believing. Sandra, don't mess with those masks. Why don't you get a hand from Midwinter as he's here?'

Martha shuddered and shook her head. She warmed her hands on her mug. Sally had been studying her.

'You're down, aren't you? If you ask me, you're alone too much. For our sort that's no good. You've got the sadness?'

'Perhaps I have.'

Martha smiled and pulled on her cloak.

'Well, thank you.'

'Any time.'

She walked back home faster than she had come. Something about that small room, the three women, had horrified her. She had smelled spite and mean tricks, gossip served hot by cold hearts.

All the same, Martha had made up her mind.

As the autumn dusk closed in Martha stood at her tall window and raised her arms.

THIRTEEN

'Trick or treat?'

Jason's fox mask made Molly jump.

'Please. It's not even Hallowe'en —' The fox-face continued to grin. 'Sorry, darling.'

'I can't find my tortoise. Will it die like the snake?'

(Die.)

Molly put her hand to her eye. Coming back from the funeral she had stumbled halfway up the hill, nearly fallen. There was a dark triangle across the corner of her eye, like a torn retina, or a gull's wing. First that prick again, then the edge of darkness. That was a week ago. Perhaps she had been rubbing where it pricked. If she left her eye alone it would go away.

Jason's expression was one of complete confidence in Molly's verdict. What terrible powers people have over each other, she thought.

'I should think it's hibernating. It's gone to sleep for the winter somewhere. It'll wake up in the spring.'

'How long will that be?'

(Forever. Endless night.)

Standing at the sink Molly looked up at the sky. She had noticed as the moon waxed the weather's temper worsened. At the moment, not quite half-moon, a leaking grey sky ran into the sea. It seemed impossible that the sun still shone above in the jet stream where the aircraft flew (Concorde shook their windows every night), unlikely that it would ever return. That is, she could not imagine it.

'Just a few months.'

Jason tried to envisage a few months.

'Will that be after Christmas?'

'Yes.'

Jason nodded and trailed out to the backyard. He seemed to make up his mind and set off along the cliffs. Enoch rose from his place by the water-butt and followed. Molly reached for the catch to open the window, to say take care, when the dizziness caught her. The sink lurched, she clung to the edge until she had her balance again and could sit down. She put her head between her legs, then sat up and breathed deeply.

The clock had righted itself on the mantel-shelf. The world continued to tick. Molly felt herself breathe normally again and yet remained abnormally aware of her breathing as if this simple capacity might at any moment be snatched from her.

Absurd. Nerves. At any rate, whatever it was, something she knew with an extraordinary certainty, was that she must fight.

The damp got into the bones, the brain, the heart. Walter's back. Norah's grief. The telephone. The fabric of houses sweated inside. The contrivances of fungus were elaborate.

Tinker said he would wash the walls with bleach but lately he had hardly been home. Molly, who had never expected him to stay, now missed him more than she would have believed possible. Gladys said he had started staying out for nights on end while Molly was ill.

'In with a bad lot,' she said, plonking down a bleeding half-carcass, Menhenniot's tribute. 'That Selina.'

'I thought she was your friend?'

'She's witched him. That's what she's done.'

'Oh, Gladys –'

'Made him silly.'

'Silly?'

'Back room of the Compass Rose. After hours. You'd never credit what goes on.'

Molly opened her mouth to ask Gladys what went on and how she knew but she felt too tired to pursue the question. Besides, Gladys remained, even in metamorphosis, a gingery person.

And I could say more, thought Gladys to herself, if I wanted to. About succubi. About people who sucked souls out of other people.

They were, in any case, interrupted. The maroon went off. They counted. Once for coastguard. Then again. Twice for lifeboat.

Nothing was found. The search was resumed the next day. Rumours ran like little devils round the town. Another fisherman dragged overboard, fatally meshed in his own trawl-net? Quarrel between brothers? Suicide? Murder? Lost with all hands?

Pouring the tea, Norah said: 'We are very close to death here.' She smiled. 'By the sea, I mean.'

Molly had decided to behave as though nothing had happened. (Well, nothing had happened, nothing you could put your finger on.) She had done her hair, put on her face and gone to see Norah. Who was sitting among her tea-cups with her hands in her lap. Dry-eyed.

'I thought I might sell them. The Crown Derby. Silly for one. Then I thought, I mustn't pack up my life yet. They're letting me stay on, you know, after all. It was Gerald they minded. It's so good to see you, my dear. The comforters have been rather a strain. They mean well but they don't know how to do it. Help me cry. I must, I know. I shall, soon.'

'I think you're very brave.'

'Well. Never mind that. Oh dear, it's raining again. Daphne Mount's nagging me to go to that dinner night. The witch man's talk. Mr Midwinter. Says it would do me good.'

'Perhaps it would.'

'We never got used to the damp. Well, it was wet out there, some of the places, but that was different. Of course, we were younger. When there was a typhoon once in Hong Kong we nailed everything up and didn't go out for more than a week. No light. No telephone. The servants didn't come in. But it was fun. I remember that. And after it rained everything was twice as beautiful. Susan wanted to come but I said no. If we took our leave in the rainy season there was mildew on everything when we got back. Oh, do you have to go?'

'It's getting dark.'

In the half-light of the tiny room Molly pulled on her oilskin with difficulty. Not much and yet so much in a small space she was afraid of breaking something.

An awkward embrace. Then Norah's voice from the darkness.

'They don't know. You won't tell them, will you?'

'Tell them?'

'That he's still here. Gerald.'

Rain. Early curtains were drawn, swish, against it but it found its way round. A place built on water. Streams ran underground, through the older, nearly-buried town, the one Martha knew. As did Fenny Trevanion. Torches blazed against streaming walls calling up shades that smelled more substantial than today's temporary lodgers. A chatter, a shout, so many voices, tongues, deaths, vital lives. The scrape of a barrel, a laugh, a scuffling, a scream, a murder. The sigh of an ordinary death, the creak of Charon's oars ferrying the living dead a short way across the water to the Plague House. Laughter.

'Look!' Martha whispered. Walter lay curled against her, his head in her hot lap, and saw through that one vision to another of an eternal forest: innocent, dangerous, forbidden. Then the walls grew fluid again and he buried his head in her fur against the silence of the aftertime.

Now was enough. They sat each side of the heaped fire and picnicked.

'Treat or trick?' Martha said feeding him from her own beak like a bird but with more favourite foods.

'Tell me again.'

Martha lit a cigarette, shifted to a more comfortable position.

Walter would never have believed he could grow to love that sulphurous breath.

'We were born,' she said, 'in Aleppo, and as soon as we were weaned the house was full of suitors. My father was in the skin trade. Even then our natures were apparent: Judith fell at once in love, Morwena drove them mad. I preferred to read and to ride. At least that was one of our births.'

'Who is Midwinter?'

'No one I want to talk about at the moment.'

Martha dipped her head to kiss the grey whorl of hair on

Walter's chest. She ran a finger down to his fork. Unclothed, Walter was the most naked man she had seen. Guardless.

'And now I'll show you a trick.'

'Where did you learn that?'

'Japan.'

Martha grinned. Walter gasped then yelled.

'No. Look. Like this.'

'I can't.' He yelled again, this time there was no mistaking his cry.

'Your back?'

He grunted yes. It was painful even to breathe. Martha stood up and surveyed him, planted on all fours.

'Damn.'

Molly again, she supposed. What a pathetic thing was this human guilt.

She coaxed, manipulated, but even with her probing of the cabbalistic spots it was all Walter could do to dress and stand up, wincing.

When he had limped off into the rain Martha paced the room, naked, chewing her knuckles. She flung herself onto her day-bed and lay back.

The little cat plopped onto her stomach and settled where Walter's head had so lately lain.

'Well, Pounce, what do we do?'

'Black is it today? Are we widowed?'

Midwinter, propped against pillows in his canopied bed, raised his eyebrows at Martha's sudden appearance. A welcome distraction. He had been working on his notes for the Dinner Club talk and the bed was strewn with books and papers.

'Are you ill?'

'Not in absolutely top form. Morwena and her bitches are after me, you know. I suppose you couldn't possibly call her off?'

'I want your advice.'

'Then don't snarl at me. I thought you said I had lost my touch?'

Martha bit her lip. She sat down, attempting to compose

herself. The room, though it was tidy and clean enough, smelled even fouler than before, as if there might be a rat dead in the wainscot. She talked. Midwinter listened and when she had finished tapped his yellowed teeth with his Gold Cross pen.

'Mmn. Well, at least you have your malice back. That's something. You should have come to me in the first place. When you mix with civilians there are bound to be complications. Sit down, sit down, woman! So impatient. The trouble is, I think, you have gone for the body but overlooked the vital organ.'

'And what's that?'

Midwinter raised one dropsically swollen finger to his skull.

'The mind, my child. The softest tissue of all. So sweet to probe. Oh dear, must you really go? I get so little company nowadays. The Principessa is a darling but she never speaks.'

'A virtue in women, surely?'

'You were always the exception, Martha. Not just one little game?'

'I've had enough of your games. They cost me my womb.' (And my child. A child. Whatever it would have been. I had such horrors. Then on the soiled sheet it was no more than a curled fish.)

'I was thinking of Mah Jong.'

No one saw Martha arrive or leave though Norah, on her way to dinner (on Wednesday she still ate liver at the out-of-season table with the view), shivered at a rush of cold air. Someone must have left a window open.

As the moon grew fat as butter Poltrue closed its summer face. The Treasure Chest opened mornings only for the sale of seasonal novelties (Hallowe'en masks, scarlet candles, and Christmas cards for the RNLI). Menhenniot, Meat Surgeon, stayed open, as did the fishmonger, the dairy, the Lobster Pot and the delicatessen.

Without the nose-to-tail cars the streets were given back to the town. Here, and in the darkening lanes of Poltreth, rumour and fact ran together in harness, swopping tales, telling stories, never short of idle ears and mouths to tell the tale again.

The Beast of the Moor made his annual return. Sheep, dogs,

cats, rabbits, were found inventively mauled to death. Tracks in the mud were indistinct but the large prints matched neither man nor any animal known to man.

Farmers armed themselves against it, organised hunts. Cottagers on the moor brought their pets in before dusk, locked their doors, closed their shutters, turned the telly on.

Molly thought of Stan and shuddered for Penny. Her mind's eye, which had grown alarmingly active lately, saw Stan, now entirely covered with a ruggy pelt, ranging the moor on all fours, fangs dripping blood. She also saw the hideous eel, the great worm reported that autumn by fishermen to be swimming just below the surface of the ocean. It swam through her dreams, with carbuncled body and crested, waving head.

While Molly's sight was better, or, at least, no worse, that inner eye saw through the skin of things. The illusion of reality shifted, so that the cobbled lanes of Poltreth between houses narrowed further still until she was afraid to enter them. The intimations that had troubled her in the spring returned but now the whispers were inside her head, cold voices urging her to the precipitous cliff-top from which it would have been so simple, so tempting, to tumble. Windows became watching squints, full of spite. Familiar faces, pulled out of shape, were masks of flesh below which maggots feasted. Death whipped through the alleys, followed her onto the ferry, was in every mouth. She fled to brighter Poltrue but even here, in the cheerful shops the lights were too bright, the shadows deep and black, the gossip of rampant tumours, fatal strokes, throats cut on safety razors, the doctor said, they cut it out but it came back, a year to live, stillborn, her own hand.

Norah mouthed at her. Molly could not hear the clink of the tea-cup. She saw through glass. Ladies' Dinner Night, Norah said and the windows of the tower above the Ocean Suite imploded, the tower toppled, chimney-pots kill.

'Ma! Ma, are you all right?'

Tinker?

Tinker found her on the cliff-top, the very edge, just one step. Gladys's wagging head, pebble glasses.

After the doctor and the pills the glass became water. Molly made herself very small so that no one would notice. She taught herself to smile and to pretend to eat. She walked by looking at the ground, holding onto walls, letting her feet take turns, one, two. She was the flat-eyed pollack in the aquarium. She could say what she liked and no one heard because there was no sound, just her mouth moving. They won't let Jason near me. The man she understood to be her husband hovered, in pain apparently. Go back to your whore, the witch, leave me alone. Worried faces (shock treatment? last resort. Keep her on her feet. Not alone.) Jason's hand on hers. Granny? His eyes large and bright with worry. If she could have reached out she would have held him in her arms. If she could have wept, she would.

'Really, darling, I'm all right. I'm going out tonight. Look at my evening dress!'

A couple of extra pills and there was hardly any pain. Molly let clucking Gladys dress her in something new from Elsie's. Gladys would take her. Gladys combed Molly's hair. Her hair hurt. Gladys tugged all the harder. Ginger woman.

'Tess has rung every day.' I won't talk to Tess. I had a friend. I've forgotten.

(Knife, cliff, fire, pills.) Tinker is building a fire near the compost heap. There will be fires.

There is a witch in every woman.

Martha!

It was a cold crossing. Molly was above them all, above herself. By the light of the full moon she looked down and saw the little boat bucking the waves, the huddled passengers in their thin packages of flesh and skin and clothes, so frail.

All Saints, thought Norah, slipping the pearls over her head, messing her hair, wondering if that powder was too white. All Saints, she said aloud, and, pulling the dead hairs from her comb, saw them all rising from their graves, shrugging off their clumsy shrouds and stepping out calmly, mingling each with the other, healed and mended. Forgiving each other, embracing. Sins shriven, love withheld now given, words that should have been spoken at last uttered. Some strolled with heads bowed, deep in conversation; others looked up and their faces were beautiful.

'Trickortreat?'

'Just try,' said Martha at the sixth ringing of the bell. The gang of variously masked small figures stopped giggling suddenly, paused speechless and at a nudge from their leader ran in the rising wind no matter where, as far as they could get from Martha's doorstep. Martha turned back to Walter.

'So Molly's ill?'

'All Hallows or Hallowe'en,' Midwinter adjusted the microphone and looked down at his audience, gathered in the former ballroom of the Channel Hotel. 'Known otherwise by the fearful as All Saints.'

He took in with distaste the view of ageing female flesh only too generously exposed: a sight he found all the more repugnant since he himself had had recourse to powder and paint. Selina, Sally and Sandra had helped him tonight, giggling around his dressing-table. At least it was something to know that he could still command acolytes. Selina had done a good job with the Leichner, not only covering the burn-scar but highlighting his better points – the set of his eyes, his cheekbones – to distract from the wattles and the waxy pallor of his complexion. The hairdresser child Sandra had wrought nothing less than a miracle, tinting not only his hair but his eyebrows so that once he was dressed in the black suit with the silky sheen Sally had so tenderly taken in, pressed and brushed and tweaked, Midwinter had surveyed in the mirror the picture of himself restored to his prime.

'Oh how lucky you are,' the girls had cried, 'to have a reflection!' and clapped their hands. There was a time he would have sported with all three not once but thrice and three times thrice. Called in his lovely boys and silky beasts.

As he heard his voice run on, giving the audience their fill of sabbats and covens, transmogrification into beasts, the fascinating habits of the Navajo and the Azande, Midwinter saw the girls sitting in the front row, Selina nudging Sandra and Sally winking, and wondered how long it would be before they sensed the extent of his weakness and first with a pinch, then with tooth and claw, tore him apart. Who would ever have dreamed that he – the great I Am who had teased the Egyptians and the Children of Israel alike – might grow old? Pupil and victim usurp the teacher's role? He who had the kingdoms of the earth in his gift to offer Christ himself.

Well, he could still hold an audience – though there seemed to be some kind of disturbance, a figure trying to rise, being held down. And where was Martha? For her he would have given up much wickedness.

Midwinter summoned for them – though not quite in the flesh – Dianus, the two-horned god. Spoke of the old, true faith, though with the deprecating half-smile of the lecturer. Such horrors he could have given them, such visions of the end even now approaching! He knew better though than to scare the customers who would ask for his signature in every one of those temptingly stacked, black and silver jacketed books.

Was that a wind getting up? Indoors? The chandelier shaking its two hundred glass tears?

'Call him Lucifer,' Midwinter concluded at his most caressing, 'Dianus, Jehovah, Allah, Beelzebub, Baal' – the chandelier groaned, the struggling figure ran from the room, the swing-door banged behind her, the air rushed out – 'the Devil himself. His were the witches. Each his handmaiden.' And up yours, Morwena dear.

As Midwinter clutched the stalk of the microphone and then his throat and Sally, Selina and Sandra rushed to surround and support him, Molly shrugged off Norah, pulled herself with unusual strength even from Gladys's grasp, and ran, the swing-door banging behind her, into a night full of noises and swooping shapes. A strange wind blew not from behind nor before but from above, sucked up every frail thing: leaves, guttery rubbish, small birds, almost Molly herself as she ran through the swing-doors, down the stairs, out of the Channel Hotel, down the road. By the time she reached the door she sought her dress was in rags.

Since Walter's back had floored him, Martha made love to him. She knew herself to be at her most powerful and wondered why (the doorbell rang) even for a second she hesitated to put her lips to his and suck out his soul. Was that the doorbell? She would put his soul in a gourd and keep it under her bed. Whatever held her back? Some scruple? The sight of her reflection in the dark, uncurtained glass?

For the seventh time that night the bell rang.

Martha flung open the door.

'Trick or treat?' Molly screamed and reaching perhaps to claw her face, fainted in Martha's arms.

That night the air was full of spirits. Bonfires were seen that had never been lit or not for a hundred years. A small fishing vessel disappeared upwards. Fish drowned in their own element. Widows lost their roofs, wives husbands and cats, a mother her child.

On the moor trees were plucked out by their roots from the ground, buzzards from their branches, the roof from the byre where Penny sheltered with Stan. A dark shape with low-slung belly loped by. In the morning a sheep was found, carcass whole, skinned. Penny clung to Stan and decided to marry him. They celebrated.

Enoch barked at the full moon as round as Penny's belly would be nine months from now.

Tinker, tending his fire, saw Selina riding the air in awful guise and rubbed his eyes.

And there were kindlier, graver souls who came from the earth and the moor and the sea to warm themselves for the last time before winter, at home.

'Gerald?' said Norah Carteret.

She took off her pearls and her dress and her flesh and her bones and went gladly to join him.

FOURTEEN

Martha Price stoked the boiler, double-locked the door, pulled down the blinds and sat cross-legged on the floor among her distracted papers. Pounce had been playing with them and scattered them into confusion but Martha found the one she was looking for. Richard Rashlay's last note, written months after Fenny had hanged and he had submitted his witness. A private scrawl, accidentally preserved, it was hard to de-cipher: 'At the last moment so She did repent, I do Believe. If there be a God may He pity her. If there be no Power and so no Sense to all our Lives, nor Reason, nor Hope, nor Wor-ship, nor Immortalitie, yet I shall hope still that her Soul went Free.'

Martha fingered her serpentine necklace, bit her lip, stood and stepped across her papers to the treasure chest in the dark corner. She had almost forgotten it. So much dust, a scent of Lebanese cedar and, within, the pickings of so many lives. A dowry of jewels scampered from her fingers, an adamantine frog bulged its sapphire eyes, velvets trembled, silks hissed and the mirror leapt into her hand.

Pounce froze in mid-wash, one leg still extended, watched as Martha gazed and saw in the glass the tracing of first one high cheekbone then the other, now a wide mouth, dark, deep-set eyes, and long hair that could never be cut. The cat followed, tail high, tip twitching, as Martha made her way up to the sleeping gallery and the cheval mirror she had bought for the pretty frame. Never in this house had it ever held a reflection until today. Pounce disapproved. Martha stood transfixed. Shed her shawl and her skirt and all her coverings until there she was: a woman naked, tall, sloping-breasted but still full, narrow hips, strong thighs and legs; sharp shoulders, belly wounded but flat enough.

The wound reminded her not so much of the womb taken from her but of another loss. The herbal abortifacts she had gathered herself, herself distilled and swallowed to expel whatever child Midwinter had so carelessly (wilfully?) given her.

What would it have become, that little fish curled on the bloody sheet? Martha, strongest of women, trembled. She touched the serpentine necklace, burned her finger-tips, sank down on her bed, put out the light. She woke in darkness. Was this it? To become human? A narrow bed in a cold house?

Martha flung her shawl over the glass, ran downstairs, tossed the hand-mirror back into the chest, slammed down the lid.

Then she stood at the blind window and touched her face in wonder and horror. Was that a tear?

In this land of no seasons Hallowe'en had for once marked the first sign of winter. A bitter east wind from Siberia dumped snow on Essex that would lie till May and further west drove Penny and Stan from the moor, banished the widows from the Promenade, found out the many cracks in the coastguard cottage – on its cliff-top so vulnerable to weather from all quarters. There was a small dog warning and the poodles of Poltrue donned coats. Those who turned out from the club for Norah Carteret's funeral were glad this was to be a cremation. Gravesides were killing cold. Among the many who wished for a westerly, however wet, were the witches. Sally, Selina and Sandra climbed to the highest point, reached out to sea, but their tricks froze in their fingers. Sadness was upon them, had been laying claim to their cold hearts since Midwinter's collapse. Sandra's silver-tinted crest drooped, Sally grew fat and white as lard, her summer bloom blown away. Tinker no longer lay with Selina in the room behind the Compass Rose. Her skinniness had turned to scrawn, her bones and temper to knives. Her pointed nose dripped. Midwinter lay in his bed in the tower of the Channel Hotel. Neither Armageddon to come – not the great cloud of death that would spring from the desert and flower most beautifully – nor any of his knowledge consoled him. He could bear only the company of the Principessa, who had entirely lost the use of her legs and was carried up once a day to sit at the head of his bed. She never spoke. It was possible that she hardly existed at all beneath the silk wrappings and cashmere shawls.

In the coastguard cottage Tinker and Stan sawed and plumbed, restored the roof as well as they could, daily replaced slates, attempted insulation, fed the ravenous fire while Penny took up her knitting again and her twins as cheerfully as she had left them. Enoch – who had at last consented to enter the house and become for the time being a hearth-dog – was hero. The night of Hallowe'en he had barked at Tinker's bonfire in a frenzy so unusual that Tinker had damped the flames with earth and saved Jason's tortoise from cremation. The reptile had found a more suitable place for hibernation in the former house of the snake beneath the compost heap. Jason was worried. He visited at least once a day with tomatoes, slices of apple and pear, then once a week until he forgot.

It was gingery Gladys who kept them all going. While Walter knelt, his back knifed in half in guilt or penitence, at Molly's bedside, Gladys bustled and hummed, cooked hotpots, simmered soup, did wonders with bones, kept Molly breathing on junket and saved Menhenniot's prime cuts for Walter.

Not that he ever ate more than a scrap.

While Gladys clucked and whistled and changed Molly's sheets and plumped up her pillow and rubbed liniment into Walter's back, Walter spent twenty-three out of twenty-four hours at Molly's bed. He snatched sleep on the floor, waiting always for the few moments when Molly roused from her sedation.

'No need for that,' Gladys had announced when Molly was taken from Martha's door to the Cottage Hospital and then to another, grimmer place where pain came in with the tide and waxed with the moon.

If only for Walter's sake (he had slept the first night on the asylum doorstep), Gladys had said Molly's best place was home, rest the finest cure. It was she who ground the pills and hid them in the junket, she who said sleep.

Gladys   grated   on   Molly's   rare   moments   of   semiconsciousness. The hand that fluffed the pillow was rough with the bedpan. Molly put on the face of sleep and tried to remember her rage. But her body became her house, her tormented mind huddled in a corner sucking its thumb while a wind whipped through her fragile frame, walls dissolved, foundations slid towards the cliff-edge. She assumed a foetal position and lay in the amniotic sac in her mother's womb, fearing to be born.

From a great distance Molly saw Tess's face disapproving of something. Her voice went on and on until Gladys switched it off.

'Off with you,' Gladys said, Hoovering Walter out of the house. He was helping no one and making himself ill.

Gingerly, his back reminding him at every step, he made his way down to the quay. He blinked at the light. He took *Cleo* out into the midstream and sat there shivering, dipping his oars against the tide to stay in one place. On the Poltreth side guilt, in the shape of Enoch, awaited his return. On the other Martha's terrace beckoned and her bed. Or was that love, grey-muzzled and patient on the quay? In which case, what had it been with Martha?

Why was he in such pain?

Pipes froze. There were undetected cracks that would later burst.

Apart from his anxiety, Walter felt strange, as though some limb long atrophied were stirring.

Walter was frightened, not just for Molly. It seemed to him, in midstream between Molly and Martha, alarming that anyone should have such dominion over another. He over Molly. Molly and Martha over him. He remembered, as though it had happened a long time ago, the splendour of that first sail in *Cleo*, the suddenness with which the ocean had changed its temper. Looking now out through the harbour mouth he saw beneath a sky of the most tender and dangerous lemon an iron sea, banded on the horizon with a streak of silver.

So calm, so cold, so flat. Walter saw how placidly the waters closed over their prey, held their secrets, casually disgorging, months, years later, the useless parcels of the dead. They took what they wanted, worked on it, spat out the rest.

Penny was waiting with Enoch on the quay.

'Pa, you're frozen.' She slipped her arm in his. 'Come on.'

Molly had woken. Gladys had propped her against pillows, almost sitting up. Her mouth moved awkwardly, taking a few sips of the soup Walter offered her. She sighed and closed her eyes. Walter had not realised how thin she had become.

When she spoke she thought she was shouting but she only whispered: 'Martha.'

The moment Martha opened the terrace door to Walter she saw that he had understood her nature.

He had rowed over through a mist that wiped Poltreth from the face of the earth. The harbour mouth was gone, the sky, Poltrue. For a while he was lost, the only sound his own breathing and the creak and dip of the oars. Then he felt the edge of the Poltrue whirlpool and Martha's landing miraculously formed, the slippery steps, the terrace. Martha saw him coming. She cracked her fingers. She still had the power. For a moment she was tempted to leave him (she had her own problems) but at last reached out and for the second time summoned him from the whirlpool.

'You have to save her,' he said.

Martha's depression was of the colour of fog. The stove roared but within her aura Martha shivered and smoked. She wore a long grey gown. She was unutterably lonely. She held Walter's face between her hands and kissed him on the lips so that for that time they both stood within her sadness. Then she let him go.

Walter said: 'I don't understand the pain.'

'That's feeling.'

'You?'

'The same.' She had retreated to the other side of the stove. He could hardly see her. She had almost become one of the tall shadows that lay in puddles on the floor, sighed against the walls and joined hands above his head where the pointy ceiling was lost in cobweb and darkness. Though her voice, with the cracked smile, was unchanged.

'It's hard to imagine them but they do exist. Love and repentance.'

'But what about Molly? You said only someone who believes can be enchanted.'

'Or loves.'

He remembered the summer. The women on the terrace, how beautiful they had been together.

Martha could still feel the power in her fingertips. She parted the mist for Walter and when he was gone called up Pounce. With her cat at her heels she walked out onto her terrace. She pointed her finger and at that moment Molly woke, smiled and asked for food.

FIFTEEN

In that phantom January spring that comes sometimes to this country, Molly healed and on Walter's arm walked in the woods among the early wild violets.

Even Midwinter, powdered and painted, allowed what was left of him to be carried by the Principessa's attendants to her basket wheelchair in a sheltered spot on the lawn. Morwena had seen his condition and dropped the libel suit. The fun seemed to have gone out of it.

Then the cold returned, snap, overnight, and snow fell, covering Gerald's grave, quieting the town across the water and the village, sending the baby snakes that would turn into a plague in the true spring, sidewinding back into the compost heap. Enoch became a white dog, a dog of snow, melting before their eyes in front of the fire.

Martha saw the image of the gulls, muted, drift diagonally across her window among the big, cold flakes. She thought this was the moment.

Martha uncovered her mirrors, recognised her reflection and wept. She took her scissors, snipped at her hair and found it could be cut.

Martha, in repentance, stepped onto her terrace. She dismissed her angry cat, took her papers – all of them, even from the locked drawer and from the testimony of Fenny Trevanion – and cast them among the snowflakes. She pulled off her serpentine necklace and flung it into the sea.

The arrival of the true spring – an exceptionally warm first week in May – found them all not so much changed, after all.

Walter had done his winter's penitence, hardly leaving Molly's side. As she grew stronger, so did his back mend. He brought her early daffodils. He found a sheltered spot where, on a good day, he settled her, wrapped in rugs, with her pad and paints. He would sit beside her for hours, his hand on Enoch's head. If she dropped so much as a hairpin he would pick it up. He thought less and less of Martha, of his summer's enchantment, but marvelled instead that this remarkable woman should be his wife, should have suffered so on his account.

Then one day before he even opened his eyes, Walter snuffed the wind from the south. Flowers? Fish? From the window he could see the blue and green water, the small waves tipped with diamonds, the ferry, the sailing boats bounding out, the fishing vessels steaming in with their silver haul, pursued by a cloud of summer gulls. The sea had regained its innocence. Molly was still sleeping. Walter pulled on his clothes, and ran down to the quay.

The first day of summer Midwinter left behind in his canopied bed the putrefying flesh and painted face. Even as the doctor covered his mouth with a handkerchief and shook his head and the Principessa sighed in a flutter of chiffon, a jackal raised its head and howled in the desert air. Snouted Set smiled. Anubis barked his welcome and the pack came from all parts, gathering for the last run.

'Oh, look, there's Walter in *Cleo* going out.'

Molly sat on Martha's terrace. Gladys joined them sometimes with her macramé.

'What happened to your cat?'

'Sally had him.'

Molly nodded. She stepped back from the easel. It was too hot to paint. For a month she had been working on a portrait of Martha.

'You can move now.'

Martha stood and stretched. Her grey aura had left her entirely along with so much else. In the course of the winter her hair had turned white. She could have cut it now but she chose not to. For the portrait she wore a long red skirt. Since she put away all her works she had taken a lover in the normal fashion and launched, with Judith's permission, her own range of home-made face creams. The smell in the house was no longer of fish smoking but of cucumber and primrose, honey and apricot.

The sisterhood between the two women was very strong.

Martha yawned.

'A drink, something long and cool?'

'Oh yes.'

Martha smiled, plucked a sprig of mint from the pot by the wall, reached up to touch her vine and stepped indoors, trailing behind her her red skirt and the long shadow that appeared in the painting, too, as a mild puddle, and accompanied her nowadays everywhere there was light enough.

JANICE ELLIOTT

THE ITALIAN LESSON

The Castello of San Salvatore is an exclusive and enchanted holiday place set in the hills above Florence and far removed from the dangerous real world below. It is just the spot for polytechnic lecturer William Farmer to pursue his search for E. M. Forster and for his wife Fanny to get over a recent stillbirth. Just the setting, too, for some wicked observation of cultural pretensions and a host of kindly but wildly funny creations.

Janice Elliott manipulates her characters and her plot with a masterly and light touch. THE ITALIAN LESSON is a wry and clever novel about the British abroad, at once a modern reworking of Forster's themes and, at the same time, strikingly original.

'There is no doubt in my mind that she is one of the most resourceful and imaginative living English novelists'
Paul Bailey in The Evening Standard

'Janice Elliott has written an elegant comedy that conceals on every page an unexploded bomb of disaster. Her interlocking events seem at first both sunny and funny – yet below the surface lurks pain and revelation. A memorable book that lingers on'
David Hughes in The Mail on Sunday

sceptre

JANICE ELLIOTT

THE NOISE FROM THE ZOO

In these, the best of her short stories which include the new 'No Man's Land', Janice Elliott explores a range of themes with all the dark wit and magic found in her novels. Combining a menacing world of the imagination with sharp observation of everyday foibles, she blends the beautiful with the grotesque, humour with tragedy, and provides a collection of stories as subtly thought-provoking as they are entertaining.

'One to my taste, dealing in smallnesses that stay small but become magical by her attention to them and the skill of her writing'
The Guardian

'We are drawn into Janice Elliott's quirky tales as much by the intriguing plots as her lucid style, her sly, inviting tone'
The Financial Times

'Manifests a fine intermittent touch for disturbed idylls and smashed arcadias'
The Observer

'Completely unpredictable . . . a gem of a collection, packed with individual jewels'
The Oxford Times

JANICE ELLIOTT

NECESSARY RITES

To Moira Frankland, writer of fairy tales, all seems in order for Christmas: her marriage works, her teenage son is reasonably civilised, and she has agreed to take in a homeless waif over the holiday. But ten years ago the couple's daughter drowned, leaving deep, unresolved grief. Her husband's MoD contract becomes worryingly sinister, and the presence of a strange girl in the house proves just as disturbing. Only young Sam perceives that his parents are making a terrible mistake.

'Achieves the tantalising dovetail between literal and metaphorical, inner and outer, that is typical of Elliott's literary agility . . . The kind of magic she always gives . . . imbues even a menacing futuristic world with beauty as well as danger'
Times Literary Supplement

'Janice Elliott is always perceptive, inventive, stylish . . . The freshness is in the adroit interlocking of the domestic and political, realistic and imaginative, childhood and maturity, through finely controlled evocation and imagery'
Daily Telegraph

'Elliott has skilfully woven the troubled state of the family with that of the nation'
Options

'The language is spare, taut and vivid . . . no opportunity for significance is wasted'
The Scotsman

'One of the most resourceful and imaginative living English novelists'
Paul Bailey

JANICE ELLIOTT

DR GRUBER'S DAUGHTER

'A delicious parade of the sinister'
David Hughes in The Mail on Sunday

'A beautifully written *tour de force* about German illegal
immigrants living with an horrendous secret in a suburban
rooming house in a city like Oxford . . . the time is 1953,
Coronation year . . . Miss Elliott's prose is as sharp and as
scintillant as diamonds'
Patrick Skene Catling in the Sunday Telegraph

'Miss Elliott is one of the most accomplished literary stylists
at work in this country, with an imagination second to none
. . . She writes like an angel. Her imagination is diabolical'
John Nicholson in The Times

'This is very well done . . . I finished the book with
considerable admiration for her insight'
Anita Brookner in The Spectator

'Janice Elliott writes beautifully . . . A fine imaginary feat'
Harriet Waugh in The Illustrated London News

sceptre

JANICE ELLIOTT

LIFE ON THE NILE

'The English in Egypt is the subject of Janice Elliott's new novel, the latest in a line of elegant and ambitious fictions. She tells the stories of two women – one a modern tourist, the other the wife of a colonial administrator in the 1920s – making use of their particular but symbolic experiences to provide an emotional history of the relationship between the two countries. Elliott makes both present and past vivid by means of powerful impressions and images which cut across time . . . she introduces an awareness of death-in-life which hovers over tombs and pleasure boats with equal menace . . . formal, literary, compassionate'
The Times Literary Supplement

' A mystery story on several levels which Elliott probes with the delicacy of an archaeologist . . . As you read the quiet title fills with colour and noise and acquires meaning. The physical sense of Egypt is directly, unobtrusively conveyed . . . The air is full of shadows and echoes'
Candia McWilliam in The Glasgow Herald

'The plot rolls from revelation to revelation until the truth has its cathartic effect. This is a stylish and imaginative book, concerned with death but also full of life'
The Sunday Times

sceptre